Ishrat Syed and **Kalpana Swaminathan**, both surgeons, write together as **Kalpish Ratna**. They explore the interface between science and the humanities.

Their recent books are *Room 000: Narratives of the Bombay Plague* (2015), *The Secret Life of Zika Virus* (2017) and *Fat: The Body, Food and Obesity* (2018).

The protagonists of Synapse, Ratan and Ramratan Oak, debuted in the novel *The Quarantine Papers* (2010).

Also by Kalpish Ratna

Uncertain Life & Sure Death: Medicine & Mahamari in Maritime Mumbai (2008)

The Quarantine Papers (2010)

Once Upon a Hill (2012)

Room 000: Narratives of the Bombay Plague (2015)

The Secret Life of Zika Virus (2017)

Fat: The Body, Food and Obesity (2018)

SYNAPSE

•

Ratan Oak Stories

KALPISH RATNA

SPEAKING
TIGER

SPEAKING TIGER PUBLISHING PVT. LTD
4381/4, Ansari Road, Daryaganj
New Delhi 110002

First published in paperback by Speaking Tiger 2019

ISBN: 978-93-88874-81-6
eISBN: 978-93-88874-80-9

10 9 8 7 6 5 4 3 2 1

for

Afaaf

neuron, synapse, connectome

The Dream of Otto Loewi

Think of it as a space.

Hiatus. Interval.

Abyss?

Perhaps.

Blindfolded, toes clawing the edge of the precipice, its cruel intelligence ground deeper into torn flesh, pain the only purchase against gravity. Yes, it might be an abyss.

Or, is it a bridge? A bridge repeated a trillion times over and jammed in your headspace.

Skull static.

Brainstride.

Thoughtfall.

Touchtick.

Sentience.

And the chance flash of sapience.

Cognition, recognition.

Syllable. Voluble babble. Within the crafting of a word, its silence seldom heard.

Crevice, cleft, a line unzipped for speed?

Speed?

Antelope flashing on Shiva's matted coif, thought escaping the matrix of existence.

Faster, much faster than an antelope that lopes along at a mere 60 mph, synaptic speed is fastest when it is a lightning jab of electricity, a little slower when chemically considered. In the very act of measuring it, we're past it.

The synapse has erased itself. It never was.

Not space, not speed.

Emptiness?

A minuscule vacuum between membranes?

Not for a moment.

The synapse is pulsatile, tidal, respirant; jostling, bursting, restoring.

Marketplace, exchange, agora. What is the merchandise?

Chemicals. Toxins. Poisons.

Stuff that could still your heart.

As it nearly did one night in 1921, waking Otto Loewi with a sudden sensation of loss. Startled, his staring eyes raked the shadows.

Nothing stirred.

The only sound was the relentless pummel of his terrified heart. As it quietened, he realized what had woken him.

A lost beat.

A break in the rhythm.

A spinning deceleration that could have regressed to stillness, if it hadn't woken him.

Yet it had woken him, and not just from sleep, but from confusion.

He knew, even before he recollected the dream that had slowed his heart and roused him.

In his dream, he was lying on his back on a sunlit balcony.

Why was he on the floor?

The warm tiles comforted his aching back.

That's right. It was *therapy*. He was in his nightshirt. The soft sunshine induced a delicious languor, ease and the anticipation of desire.

Clouds, tender and iridescent, melted in the blue haze.

Otto recognized the underpainting of rich tints that shimmered through the cloud.

He would know that sky anywhere.

He would know that palette too.

It was the Bologna of Annibale Carracci.

Between him and the sky dangled joints of meat.

Is that where he was? In the butcher shop of Annibale Carracci?

Carracci had a thing about butchers and meat, he painted them over and over again. But his slabs and haunches were big smoky crimson hecatombs. Nothing like *these*.

These joints swinging overhead glistened blue-pink and zartgrün on shining copper hooks, whirling in a merry carousel.

Pretty, and macabre.

No goat or sheep could be so perfectly miniaturized, so delectably compacted in thigh and calf.

Birds, were they?

Rats?

Frogs.

Of course. If this was Bologna, they must be frog's legs. Galvani's frogs. Volta's frogs.

Otto waited—as a breeze lifted the frogs' legs in a grisly can-can, they touched the iron balustrade and— *jumped*.

This was Galvani's magic, this animal electricity. A jab of electric charge from the metal, and the muscle twitched.

That was how nerves worked, with a shudder of current. Hadn't they believed that for two centuries? Who was he, Otto Loewi, to say different?

Say *what*?

As if in answer, the tiny legs dripped a splotch of fluid onto his thin nightshirt.

It struck him like an icicle.

His heart dropped a beat.

Resumed.

Slowed.

S-l-o-w-e-d.

And woke him.

Was he still in the dream when he reached for his notebook to record its rapidly dissolving logic?

His pencil flew almost of its own will. He had it down, every word. And then, clutching the notebook, he fell asleep.

The notebook was lying on the floor, next to the bed, when he woke. He picked it up immediately, but put off opening it. The dream, and all it would mean to the world, frightened him. If he could have fled the moment, he would have gladly done so.

Too late now.

It had fallen to his lot, this stupendous discovery, this annunciation of greatness.

His heart was exultant, no more of that hesitant slowing the dream had induced.

Through the clench of morning, Otto kept away from his laboratory.

It was Easter Sunday, and long before dawn, already a day of miracles. Perhaps the day would pass without offering him one generous hour of solitude to read his notes, but he could wait.

Could he?

Was his unwillingness to open the notebook a delay — or dread?

What if he had merely dreamed writing down the dream?

He had no recollection, none, of what he had written. The dream he recalled very clearly, in synæsthetic detail. A shudder of pleasure trilled down his spine as he remembered the sun-warmed tiles against his skin.

What did it all *mean*?

Otto Loewi opened his notebook.

On the instant, a scream strangling his throat, helpless hands clawing the empty air, he flung it across the room.

It was all —

It was all gibberish.

There was nothing at all in the notebook — nothing but a close tedious scrawl, indecipherable and completely useless.

He remembered how he had grabbed a pencil and scratched away in the dark. He hadn't dreamt transcribing the dream — he had simply written in the dark, lines entangled, inextricable dashes and loops, cobwebs on the page.

He spent an hour, magnifying lens in hand, trying to imagine what the markings meant.

It was no use. His misery was past bearing. To come so close and lose it all…

Lose *what*?

There was no answer to that.

Eventually, Otto Loewi, much against his will, slept.

He woke again at the same hour.

The clock on the landing struck three.

He had dreamed the dream anew.

This time Otto did not hesitate. Pulling on his clothes, he rushed to his laboratory.

In the sudden blaze of light, the frogs in the tank blinked trustingly as Otto swung a hammer at two of the largest.

He scarcely noticed what he was doing as he set up the experiment, so intent was he on the unravelling meaning of his dream.

He had both frogs dissected in a trice, shining viscera exposed as if designed solely for his scrutiny.

He swiftly isolated the small hearts, elegant as jewels, one with its nerves intact, the other without.

The light went out of the two cadavers, dimming as they congealed glassily into death.

Otto set up the hearts in perfusion experiments.

The first, the one with nerves, would serve as understudy for his dream, for that was Galvani's idea. An electric shock to the nerves would alter the action of the heart.

The heart has two nerves. The lengthy vagus which wanders a long way from its root in the brain, and the sympathetic nerves drawn from the neighbour network.

A shock to the vagus would make the heart slow.

A shock to the sympathetic would make the heart race.

That much was known already, but he, Otto, was going to play out his dream.

He secured glass tubes to perfuse the hearts with saline and keep them ticking. They did so bravely, steadily, long enough for him to get a baseline trace on the revolving kymograph.

Two hearts, beating as one.

He smiled at that bit of romantic rubbish.

The heart with nerves intact, he labelled Donor. The other, Recipient.

He jabbed the vagus nerve of the Donor with a mild shock. Predictably, the Donor's pace slowed, much as his own heart had done in his dream.

Otto took a sample of the fluid perfusing the Donor, and used it to lave the Recipient.

The Recipient which had been beating merrily—paused. Slowed, just as the Donor had, when the vagus nerve was stimulated.

But this heart had no nerves!

A chemical in the perfusing fluid from the Donor had slowed it down.

This was the meaning of his dream.

The vagus nerve slowed the heart not by a shock of electricity, but by the chemical that had dripped onto him in his dream.

Absently, he named the chemical *Vagusstoff*.

What did the name matter, it was bound to be superseded.

Absently too, he repeated the experiment. This time he made the Donor race by shocking the sympathetic nerve and watching the effect of its perfusate on the Recipient.

Predictably, it raced.

So the sympathetic nerve produced another chemical?

The meaning of it all dazzled him.

The interregnum between the nerve and the heart muscle, the space British physiologists had named *synapse*, was not just an emptiness waiting for a jolt of electricity to cross it.

It was a factory that made chemicals.

These chemicals were messengers.

Slow down, or *hurry up* they had told the heart muscle.

The electric shock to the nerve had produced this intelligence.

That's what a synapse was — *intelligence*.

Otto's hand trembled, but his pen moved with assurance, propelled by the idea glimpsed in his dream:

> *A nervous impulse is transmitted to the tissue of the heart by chemical substances which may be called, and are called, chemical transmitters.*

Otto had been jolted into a place of sudden intelligence where everything oneiric had crystallized into shape and intent.

He was at the intersection between idea and act.

For years the idea had hibernated in experiments, and now surfaced in his dream.

In the sunlit balcony he was both observer and subject, for hadn't his own idea stopped his heart?

And he was here now, in that moment made tangible, holding with trembling hands the shimmer of a thought, now here, now lost.

Otto Loewi was within the synapse.

Leopold Café

When Ratan Oak looked up, the man he was expecting had arrived. He sat down against the mirror, a bullet hole above each shoulder. A third, between them, would have drilled right through his heart.

At half past nine, thirteen days ago, two men had lobbed a grenade in here, then stepped in and let loose with AK-47s.

Everyone at Leopold's this morning stared at those bullet holes, and the man got in the way. He tipped back his chair and considered their stares with polite disdain.

Ratan seemed to know why he was here—but dimly—and only in the dark looking-glass of his mind.

* * *

Ratan hadn't meant to step into Leopold Café. The signboard had caught his eye. A '50s blue-and-white Coca Cola 'good times' poster that said *Since 1871*. He hadn't noticed that before. The old one had been white, with squat black letters, and something of a memorial to Prema. Their first quarrel had erupted over that sign.

She wanted to go in. He hadn't.

'I'm not eating in a place named for a butcher,' he said.

'How do you know that? Maybe Leopold's the owner. Maybe Leopold's his uncle.'

'It is Irani, Prema. They don't have Leopolds in Yazd. It is named for Leopold of Belgium, the butcher of the Congo.'

'Why Yazd? Why not Tehran? Maybe they don't know he was a butcher, maybe they don't even know where the Congo is. Why should they? All they need to know is bun maska and chai, and that's all I want. Not everyone bothers about useless stuff, like you.'

That peripatetic quarrel had lasted nearly a decade.

Lucky they parted when they had. It had done him good.

At least he hadn't heard from her since.

They hadn't gone into the café after all, that awful day. Twenty—good heavens—twenty-six years ago. A long while, to keep a quarrel going. And all she had wanted was bun maska and chai.

Ratan entered Leopold's with the feeling of walking into a mirage. He expected the restrained grief a house of death exhibits the week after—a quiet decency, with an attention to detail that marks the return to life. Leopold's was nothing like that. It was...blasé. The cheery red-and-yellow checked table-cloth, the single rose, the slotted steel napkin holder, all disowned chaos.

It was surprisingly crowded, considering the hour. European tourists at breakfast, mostly, with the relaxed air of having checked in last night at the oasis. For all its tragic present, the café conveyed the comfort of a haven.

It felt like the last stop on the Orient Express. Empire still lingered here, and not just in the naïve mural where pink ladies chatted brightly with gentlemen in sola hats and chocolate brown waiters hovered, bearing trays.

The backpacker consulting his *Lonely Planet* and the

two French girls examining him furtively, the British couple intent on their sausages and the American woman writing postcards—they could all have been here since 1871.

The rest, all Indian, were here because of 26/11, paying the uneasy homage of curiosity when the time for aid and condolence was past.

This irritated Ratan. He bristled when the waiter pointed out the bullet holes. Nonetheless, he looked. They were in the large mirror across the room. Three holes, each nested in a bright nebula of fracture lines sucked deep into the black continuity of glass. The space beyond made the room around him shimmer. Beyond the glass everything was fungible and familiar, tangible and sentient.

Something was still missing.

It would come now, in the next ten minutes, before half past eight. Once settled in its expected place, it would alter this geometry of light and shadow. It would complete the picture, and make the place familiar again.

It wasn't unusual for Ratan to experience the familiar in an unfamiliar place. It was useless telling himself he had never been inside Leopold Café before. All he had to do was wait.

He looked away from the mirror, frowning. Fisticuffs pounded the inside of his skull. His other life, awakened, was clamouring for liberty.

The pain no longer frightened him, but he still flinched from it. Sometimes, as now, he couldn't be sure if it was pain—or excitement. Everything was heightened. Colour grew more intense, smells stronger, and vision more acute. Conversations buzzed annoyingly about him. His skin was raw with anticipation, as if the lightest touch would unleash a convulsion. Time accelerated. He was keen to enter his other life. The life of Ramratan Oak.

All he had to do was wait. He gritted his teeth and waited for the man to arrive. That was it. There should be a man at the table by the mirror. But he wasn't here yet.

The waiter took Ratan's order without comment. Why, what had he expected?

* * *

'Sorry, sir. Europeans only.'

* * *

More than a crazy thought, Ratan actually heard the words. But he couldn't have. Here came his coffee.

* * *

'I must request you to move to the back of the room.'

* * *

Ratan turned, though the waiter hadn't spoken at all. When he looked again at the mirror, the picture was complete.

The man was sitting there now, as expected. He leaned forward a little and his back loomed in the mirror, drilled neatly with a bullet hole. The spidery cracks around it radiated brightness into the space beyond.

There, in that dim interior, was Ratan's table; and there he was, stealing a glance at the man; then quickly looking away and smoothing his moustache—

His *moustache*?

Perhaps it's time I grew one, thought Ratan.

* * *

Don't. It is a—

* * *

—plant of great cultivation, Ratan finished the sentence with irony.

* * *

His own eyes twinkled back at him from the mirror as Ramratan Oak polished his spectacles to take a better look at the man. Next to Ramratan, Ernest Hanbury Hankin, shielded by a newspaper, was half-way through the man's story.

'He's growing immortal just sitting there,' murmured Hankin. 'Year by year by year every minute.'

'How can he possibly do that?'

* * *

'How can he possibly do that?' Had he just said it?

The waiter seemed to have heard him. He followed Ratan's eyes.

'Takes all sorts, doesn't it?' he said. 'That's his table, and he won't sit anywhere else. Who are we to object? He's here like clockwork, eight-fifteen, every morning. Made big noise because we were closed four days after the attack. Orders breakfast and eats in great hurry—before his friend turns up.'

'Oh, that isn't his friend.'

'No? Business contact, maybe. Not *our* business. Anything else, sir?'

Recollecting why he was here, Ratan asked for bun maska.

The waiter smiled.

'We keep changing the menu, but Indians only ask for bun maska.'

'At least these days you allow Indians. In the old days you would have refused to serve me.'

'Impossible!'

'Not to worry. Times have changed now.'

'That's good, then.'

The man looked exactly as Ratan remembered him.

* * *

Exactly as he looked now to Ramratan in the mirror.

Ramratan had polished his spectacles twice in ten minutes, as if that might help his disbelief.

Immortal? He hadn't seen anybody looking this mortal of late.

The man's face was like crumpled parchment, his pale blue eyes brilliant chips of ice. He was tall, taller than Ramratan, but with a curious laxity of limb. His large hands were covered with tortuous veins tensed in blue knots against startlingly white skin. In contrast, his white ducks looked yellow. The many layers of linen beneath his khaki jacket were limp with perspiration. He removed his sola and dabbed preciously at his beaded forehead.

* * *

Ratan noticed the man was dressed differently, in kurta pajama now. His long exquisite feet stuck out in beautifully crafted kolhapuris. In Ramratan's time it was called 'going native.'

He was waiting, as Ratan had seen him wait before—Ratan's bun maska arrived.

The waiter was a young man. He couldn't know the dish was iconic, and with it should come a syrupy cup of Irani chai. Also, it was clear Leopold no longer baked its own biscuits. In his childhood, Iranis served biscuits with their chai for free. Nankhatai, Shrewsbury, ginger, coconut—

* * *

'Coconut biscuits,' said Hankin. 'These really are the best in the world.'

Ramratan bit into one. Rough and dry, but that might just be the waiter.

'Disregard the waiter,' murmured Hankin. 'I'll break his skull for you another day.'

The thought of Ernest breaking anyone's skull made Ramratan smile. Meanwhile, the waiter had retreated, mollified by Hankin's largesse.

'There, he won't trouble us anymore. He isn't a bad man, really, Ramratan, just—'

'Just a victim of the times,' Ramratan preempted Hankin.

'Sorry I had to bring you here. You did want to see the man.'

'Yes, Ernest, I do. Forget the rest.'

He stole another look at the man near the mirror.

'How old did you say he was? He looks about a hundred to me.'

'That I can answer with accuracy. He's exactly seventy-four years, two months and two days old this morning. I've seen his papers. Patton Prescott. Born 5 October 1829.'

'Looks older.'

'He'll look younger the next time we see him. If the rumour is true.'

* * *

Ratan no longer had any doubt. This was the same man. The man Ramratan and Ernest Hankin were talking about. The man whose shoulders were on the other side of those bullet holes.

Today was 8 December, 2008.

In the mirror, Hankin was reading the *Times*. The date on

the masthead was 8 December, too. But the year was 1903. Ramratan had just turned forty and Hankin was younger. Ratan rummaged for a sense of what it had felt like then, wondering what the moment's sting had been, and why it had marked him thus, with memory.

Prescott. The man's name was Prescott.

Patton Prescott.

Could Ramratan see him through the bullet hole? Was that all it took, to be able to see through the mirror? As if in answer, Ramaratan took off his spectacles and looked at him. And, all at once, Ratan was there.

* * *

Patton Prescott had been evicted from Watson's Hotel for creating a disturbance. Naturally, Mrs Biggett took him in.

In the world of lodging houses, Biggett's had a reputation for dullness. A neat narrow building in Byculla's Clare Road, it had once been a baniya's pleasure house. Bankruptcy, and a strong attack of religion, had forced the baniya to sell the place. Mrs Biggett, recently widowed, bought it for a song. It had few graces and she ensured none of its former airs endured. There was no drunkenness, no lechery, no conversation and nothing to eat. And whenever he was in Bombay, Hankin boarded here.

'It's a well-kept secret, Ramratan, but the woman has a kind heart. I've never known her to turn away rejects. She heard of the incident at Watson's, and asked me to vet Prescott's papers. Everything seemed in order, so there was no reason to turn him away.'

In the dead hour before dinner, when Mrs Biggett serves no apéritif and hungry boarders shuffle between carom and planchette without hope, Hankin began a conversation with Prescott.

Initially, Prescott wasn't forthcoming, but it did emerge he wasn't here on a pleasure trip. He was in Bombay for his health.

'He began questioning me about native medicine. A misleading label, I told him, and—'

'—lectured him for an hour about Unani Tibb and Ayurveda—'

'I did no such thing! I merely answered his questions.'

'Right, right. Go on.'

'He was undergoing a native treatment, he said, which would be of great interest to European scientists.

'I wanted to learn more. He was reticent at first. Then said he had been given an elixir. You know, Ramratan, I'm always suspicious of terms like elixir and tonic—'

'*Bal Amrut.* Liver Pills. *Bilousine.*'

'Exactly! The market's thick with them. I asked him if he knew what this elixir was.

'"The elixir of youth," he recited with a trusting smile. It was all done very scientifically, he assured me. His doctor had shown him elixir-fed rats that were two hundred years old. He said they were tireless.'

'He meant they fucked like crazy.'

'Probably. But I don't think it was only that. He's signed up for the elixir. Said he felt twenty years younger already, and all he'd had so far was the introductory dose. "Is it a pill?" I asked. He smiled. Nothing like a pill he said. It was a curry, a delectable curry. And the coin dropped. Goat's testes! This hakim has fobbed him off with *gurda kapoora.* Have you tried it? Very popular among the bucks in Agra.'

'Here too. This nation's eaten it for centuries. Yet look at us. No. Prescott's doctor has something more exotic on offer. The next phase of therapy will probably involve rhinoceros urine.'

'Well, he did say the treatment goes from solid to liquid to gas. He's ready for the liquid phase now. The hakim administers the dose right here. Every morning at exactly half past eight.'

'Why here? And not in his dawakhana?' Ramratan posed the question, only to answer it himself. 'I suppose it would be infra dig for Prescott to visit him there.'

He stole another glance at Prescott, but couldn't for the life in him discern the faintest sign of youth.

'Why?' asked Ramratan.'Why is he doing this, Ernest?'

'I asked him that, in fact. His answer was peculiar. On his seventieth birthday he realized, at last, he was rich enough to enjoy youth.'

'Someone else's youth, you mean? Are you sure he's meeting a doctor and not a pimp?'

'Heavens, I didn't think of that!'

Hankin wouldn't, Ramratan knew. Despite his raging battle with the Indian Medical Service, Hankin could never believe the worst of his fellow men.

'So, that's the hakim!' Hankin whistled softly.

A burly man in a flowing muslin djibba and grubby churidar pajama had joined Prescott. Something about him seemed faintly familiar. His back to them, he listened to Prescott, who had a great deal to say. The red tassel on his fez swung a fraying pendulum, like time dispersed to the frequency of his approving nods.

Holding up a finger for silence, he ceremoniously measured Prescott's pulse. Charisma or coincidence, he induced absolute silence. The air seemed to congeal, and then his voice was heard.

'One drop of semen, Prescott Sahib,' he said, 'one drop of semen is equal to seven drops of blood.'

Then that finger again, cautionary, this time.

'Count your drops, Mr Prescott. Count—your—drops.'

Hankin reddened with suppressed laughter.

'Moustaches, Ernest, were invented for moments like these.'

Was Prescott embarrassed? He didn't look it. Oblivious to all else, he was tuned to the hakim, as if mesmerized.

The hakim stood up and walked around to Prescott's side of the table. A small phial gleamed in his right hand. Prescott leaned his head back and the hakim bent over him. When he stood upright again, Ramratan saw his face for the first time.

He leapt up and would have rushed at the man if Hankin hadn't gripped his arm and forced him back into his chair.

'I know this rascal!' Ramratan was furious. 'I've seen him hanging about the Mortuary. That wasn't goat he fed Prescott! Hurry, Ernest, before it's too late.'

* * *

'Anything else, sir?'

Ratan returned to the present. The bun maska sat untouched before him. He ordered another coffee to get rid of the waiter, then turned anxiously back to the table by the mirror where Prescott still awaited his guest.

In the mirror Prescott's hakim now had his back to Ratan. The phial put away, he was taking his leave.

He glanced over his shoulder and through the bullet holes into the room. His light brown eyes sparked carnelian as they focused on Ratan. He ignored Prescott's farewell and hurried out.

Ramratan and Hankin had disappeared. Only Prescott

kept his seat, back to back with his twin, on Ratan's side of the mirror.

Ratan sipped the coffee. It helped steady him. He became aware of a soreness in his calves. Odd. He'd barely walked a mile. No, not odd at all—it was very long since he'd raced on a bicycle.

* * *

He was peddling hard with Hankin weighing down the Raleigh. Still, quicker than a tram! They reached the Mortuary in half an hour.

Eight-thirty on Saturday morning. The place was deserted.

Ramratan peered into the Autopsy Room. The four cadavers from the day before lay exactly where he'd left them.

'Bhiku!' he thundered.

An alarmed clerk from the Coroner's Office popped his head out and retreated hastily.

'Bhiku!' Ramratan bellowed again, louder.

This time, Bhiku's son Mangesh slunk out. He was a gangly lad of sixteen, with a taste for chandol. Twice in the last year Ramratan had hauled him out of Liang's chandol-khana, the sleazy opium den in Safed Gali.

'Where's Bhiku?' he demanded.

'He's ill.'

'Get him! I'll cure him when he gets here.'

The boy did not budge. Last night's revels showed in his pinpoint pupils. 'He said I was to do his work today.'

Bhiku, then, was too drunk to even stand up.

Ramratan snarled and strode past the boy's inane smile.

Hankin followed him into the Autopsy Room. The air smelt of carbolic and bleached blood. Tall windows, fierce with morning, blazed over the four dead men. They stared straight up, sightless. The marble slabs gleamed in milky opalescence.

'Lock the door, Ernest!'

Ramratan was already bent over the first cadaver, a mason who had fallen off a scaffold and died on impact, the contre-coup shearing his brainstem. He looked young in death, the burden of life lifted off him.

Ramratan whispered an apology that would never be heard and dipped his hand between the man's legs to heft the scrotum. It settled cold and soft in his palm. He pressed down with his thumb. It sank right in.

Hankin met his eyes. Ramratan nodded.

So too the next. The one after. And, the last.

'All?'

'All four. Cotton wool.'

He strode out and collared Mangesh.

'Come on!'

He half-lifted, half-dragged the terrified boy, bumping his knees along the sloping corridor.

'Walk, will you? Take us there!'

Mangesh led them, as Ramratan expected, to one of those green-curtained cubicles that line the pavement on Shuklaji Street.

'He won't be here,' said Hankin. 'May still be at Leopold's.'

But Ramratan was beyond counsel.

Above the green curtain a neat sign in English announced: 'Clinic of Confidence'.

* * *

Clinic of Confidence!

Ratan laughed out loud. Why, he knew that place! He remembered staring at it from the upper deck of the 4Ltd in

Dongri. Never those local trains for him, he was a B.E.S.T. man all through his undergraduate days when traffic inched its way through Mohammad Ali Road giving him time enough to memorize the blackboard list outside the Clinic of Confidence. He recalled it now, verbatim.

Hydrocoele, piles, fistula, small size increase, weakness, lack of interest, debility, thin semen, thick semen, semen block, semen loss, all kinds of venereal diseases.

And then in tall red capitals:

LIFELONG GUARANTEE OF FULL TENSION SATISFACTION TO EXTREME OLD MEN & MIDDLE AGES
HAKIM ARIF KHAN DEHLAVI, *B.U.M.S.*

The sign was a standing joke. Nobody bothered with the hakim's name. The Medical College knew him simply as Bums & Cums.

Ratan hadn't seen that board since the flyover opened to traffic. Like many things that had lasted the century, it did not cross over into the new millennium.

But Prescott was here. Patton Prescott. He could be nobody else. It had worked then, the elixir of youth!

* * *

That wasn't how he remembered it. They had kept the elixir from Prescott, hadn't they, after they burst in on the hakim?

They dived into the Clinic of Confidence, then up a staircase. No—a ladder, wedged in a dark alcove. And above, way above, a skylight glared like a malignant ocellus. His fingers hooked onto Mangesh's collar,

Ramratan urged the boy forward as Hankin lumbered slowly behind them. They trudged up five stories to emerge on a loft right beneath the tenement rafters.

Here was no attic. This was a laboratory busy with flasks, glass tubes angled and sinuous, stout jars, alembics and shelves. Rows and rows of wooden shelves, ancient, cracked, bursting with secrets in the frigid stagnant air.

A blue flame leapt, and there he was, their quarry, and if the signboard was to be believed, Hakim Arif Khan Dehlavi. His agate eyes dilated over the wild tangle of beard as he caught sight of them.

A small alembic hissed and sputtered over the flame. In its blue flicker the table was covered with a nacreous shimmer.

It was heaped with testes—big, small, grey, pink, glistening, dull.

Gonads crowded and jostled for space, as if a massacre raged outside these walls and a maniac loosed upon the dead had cached his spoils in here.

Strange, the cold air held nothing of the feral odour of dying tissue.

All this registered in the blink before Ramratan sprang at the man. Hankin had to prise his hands off the hakim's fat neck.

'I got these from the abattoir,' the man rasped when Ramratan let go. 'There's no law against that.'

'I'll see you hanged, even if I have to do it myself,' roared Ramratan.

The hakim turned to Mangesh.

'There's no hope for you, boy, opium's got your soul.' He soothed his neck and mopped his face. 'You must be Oak Sah'b. It hasn't been easy getting past you.'

'Where's the stuff you stole from the dead?'

The hakim pointed sullenly to the alembic. Its

sinuous conduit led to the far end of the table where it dripped into a thin glass flute. Tiny amber globules condensed on its sides and rapidly filled the flute with a clear golden liquid.

Hakim Arif Khan sealed off the glass tube and held it out to Ramratan.

'Here! The essence of your dead. Take it! It has the strength of four men. Take it with my promise. I will stop making eunuchs of dead men. Out of respect for you, for I hear you treat the dead as your own.'

Ramratan hesitated.

'Take it. Arif Khan Dehlavi is, in truth, Arif Khan Barmaki. If you know what that means, you will take me at my word.'

The name meant nothing to Ramratan. Nevertheless, he took the hakim at his word. What else could he do?

'Leave Prescott to me,' said Hankin when they were out once again in sunlight. He took the test tube from Ramratan and dashed it to pieces on the pavement.

* * *

The crunch of glass jolted Ratan back to the present.

The table by the mirror now had a second occupant.

Prescott's guest had arrived.

Ratan had missed the opening act. Prescott had his face buried in his hands. His companion stood by and watched him with dispassion. Glass glittered on the floor between them.

'There!' the man said, and Ratan recognized the voice at once. 'There! That's the end of it all.'

'No!'

Ratan crossed the room in rapid strides. 'It didn't quite end like that. You didn't let him go that easily, did you? Don't you remember how it ended, Mr Prescott? Hakim Arif Khan Dehlavi didn't let you off so easily.'

They turned, not to answer him, but to follow his eyes as they focused beyond them.

In the mirror, they were back at his table. Older, much older now. Scarred. Hankin had lost most of his hair, but the moustache still bristled gallantly. And Ramratan?

Ratan saw himself, twenty years older.

The date was 8 December again. The year was 1923.

* * *

'Remember Prescott?' asked Hankin. 'Hakim Dehlavi didn't let him off easy.'

'Twenty years ago. To the day.'

'Is it? Good God!'

'Whatever happened to Prescott? You sailed home with him, didn't you? It was the end of the hakim's elixir. I certainly had no trouble with him after that.'

'No robbed cadavers?'

'Not another one. As long as I ran things there—'

'You still do.'

'No, Ernest. Not any longer. Just fingerprints. Bloodstains. Fussy stuff like that. I only do police autopsies now. Earlier, till the end of the War, I checked every single corpse myself before I released it from the Mortuary. Never missed any more testes. I put the fear of the noose in Bhiku.'

'And his son?'

'Mangesh? Dead. Never woke up from a week-long trance in Liang's chandol-khana.'

'Pity.'

Ramratan was silent. His city was built on opium. Libraries, hospitals, railway stations, and most other emblems of philanthropy—they were all built upon the wreckage of lives.

'Prescott came to a bad end, Ramratan. I am certain our hakim had everything to do with it.'

Hankin had sailed back to England with Prescott and was relieved to see him met at the pier by his son. He never saw Prescott again.

And then, last year, the name cropped up in a conversation. Prescott, he learnt, had run wild. His family, torn between embarrassment and despair, had finally ceded all hope of reforming him. He ended up in the madhouse and died gibbering in a straitjacket.

'Reformed? Did he behave like those rats he told you of? Did he run around naked? Old men do terrible things. I worry sometimes, over what lies ahead.'

'I went down to Shropshire to find out. I visited the family—a son and a daughter. I told them I'd known Prescott in Bombay. They said he'd gone to pieces a year after his return from India, reeling about drunkenly with not a drop of alcohol in him. Lost all sense of self and lasted another six months in the asylum.'

'Poor man! Ernest, could it have been something entirely unrelated? You destroyed that extract Arif Khan gave us.'

'I asked them about medication. They were quite emphatic. No, he wasn't taking medicine. Of any sort. But I can be devious too! I asked about his general health. Headaches, colds, fevers, that sort of thing.'

'Ah.'

'Exactly. He was a martyr to coryza, the daughter said, and never without his little flask of nasal drops. I was, don't forget, asking these questions nearly twenty years after. People can't be expected to remember details.'

Ramratan pondered a long while.

'Even if Prescott kept receiving supplies from the hakim, why should the elixir drive him crazy? Any daughter would elide over such embarrassments. Are you certain, Ernest, they didn't mean randy when they said mad?'

'Yes, yes. I made quite sure of that. I read all the notes at the asylum. No sexual excitement of any kind. I wondered about that *any kind!*'

'So it didn't work like that. It changed his behaviour, his mentation, and his intellect. What do testes have to do with that?'

'Men often think with theirs.'

Ramratan nodded. The War had made cynics of them all.

He couldn't let go of the story. It had happened so soon after Prescott reached England. A yammering idiot within a year and in six more months, dead. All along, he had used the elixir nasally—as swift a route as injecting the drug into a vein. It had addled Prescott's brain.

* * *

'The elixir turned you mad, didn't it, Mr Prescott?'

Prescott turned to Ratan in startled disbelief, and then laughed. 'I've never felt saner. How would you know about the elixir, anyway?'

Ratan did not reply. He had made a complete fool of himself. Prescott was *dead*. But this man—

'I think this gentleman is speaking about your grandfather, Mr Prescott,' said the hakim. 'And also, about mine.'

He scrutinized Ratan with astute eyes.

'Your name? Is it Oak?'

Ratan stared back, baffled.

'I think we better have a word, Mr Oak—or, is it *Dr* Oak? I'm almost through with Mr Prescott here. *Permanently,* through. Please? Will you give me five minutes?'

Ratan nodded, walked back to his table and pondered the physics of breaking glass. It splinters in conchoidal fractures as shock waves ripple out. This was a mirror, not a window-pane. The dark space within it, he alone could explore.

Prescott—*that* Prescott—had gone mad from the elixir. This one might too. Madness is a convenient label for all things inconvenient.

What exactly happened to Patton Prescott?

Today it would be termed dementia, poor coordination, ataxia.

A neurologist might not make the connect, but Ramratan Oak did—because he knew what the elixir really was. He lacked a name for Prescott's illness, because in his time it had no name.

He, Ratan, made the diagnosis because Prescott's illness now had a name. It was a prion disease, and the elixir had transmitted it.

Ramaratan's cadavers were never robbed again. Yet Hakim Arif had ensured that Prescott in England received enough elixir to last a year.

Hakim Arif Khan Dehlavi walked over to Ratan. He was very different from the man who had made a gift of the phial to Ramratan. His light brown eyes, though gentle and lustrous, recalled that carnelian flash. He drew up a chair and sat down next to Ratan.

'You're not Hakim Arif Khan, are you?'

'No. My name is Moinuddeen.'

'Moinuddeen Khan Dehlavi. Or, Moinuddeen Khan Barmaki?'

Moinuddeen's face lit up.

'Your grandfather knew! We were told he didn't.'

'So, it is family lore?'

Moinuddeen shrugged and suppressed a smile.

Ratan felt a lance of anger.

'The name meant nothing to Ramratan Oak, and it doesn't to me.'

'Barmaki is the ancient name of Hakims who studied medicine before Islam. Charak, Sushrut, Jalinoos. And also— the medicine of the Pharoahs.'

Something glimmered in Ratan's memory but he couldn't place it.

Moinuddeen nodded. 'I see it begins to make sense.'

* * *

A hook.

* * *

What did a hook have to do with it?

* * *

Ask him about the hook.

* * *

Ratan, compelled, asked, 'You have a hook, I suppose. I'd like to see it.'

'You knew?' Moinuddeen gaped.

'He did. Ramratan Oak, the man who met your grandfather.'

Ratan looked down. He didn't want Moinuddeen to guess what he had just realized. Vision or memory, call it what you will, he knew every word before Ramratan's broad-nibbed Waterman set it down on paper.

* * *

...I can't help thinking we were wrong all along about that elixir. I kept counting testes, I became obsessed with that, and it kept me from seeing the larger picture. It had nothing to do with testes at all.

I tell you, Ernest, it was the pituitary! Extracted with a hook, through the nostrils, in the ancient Egyptian manner. Leaving no trace of intrusion. How am I going to live this down?

Every one of those cadavers I passed as legit was missing its pituitary gland. God forgive my ignorance, because I never can.

* * *

'How many more victims, Moinuddeen?' asked Ratan quietly. 'Prescott's grandfather died mad and demented.'

Moinuddeen laughed.

'He was mad and demented to begin with, wasn't he? Look at this Prescott! You think he looks mad or demented?'

'Actually, yes. He does.'

Prescott had recovered his magisterial calm. His back obliterated the bullet holes.

'Men like Prescott live on the edge of Time,' said Moinuddeen. 'No matter what age, they're always on the edge of Time.'

'What does that mean?'

'All they see is the abyss. Nothing registers but that emptiness. Nothing is real except their terror.'

'And you cash in on it.'

'Why not? The day after the Lashkar shootout, that very morning, he was waiting for me by the door. The corpses were still here, blood everywhere. He didn't seem to notice. Nothing mattered but his fix.'

'You were here too, weren't you? Vial in hand, to offer him his fix?'

Moinuddeen lowered his eyes. 'Yes, I was. Demand and supply.'

'Why did you break the vial just now?'

'Because I broke with him.'

'Why?'

Moinuddeen shrugged and looked back at the table by the mirror. Prescott responded with a quick grimace of pain.

'Look at him. Don't you think he's lived long enough?'

'He doesn't think so,' said Ratan.

'Who is he to decide?'

'Who are you?' asked Ratan.

'I'm his timekeeper. That's who I am!'

Despite himself, Ratan asked, 'Does it work?'

'How old do you think I am?'

'Thirty-five?'

Moinuddeen smiled. Ratan noticed a craquelure of grey on his pale skin, as if its depths abjured light.

'Was that your grandfather? Mortuary Oak?'

'Great-grandfather. Dr Ramratan Oak, pathologist.'

'Your *great*-grandfather. There's your answer! Pathologist, mortician—what's the difference? They're both doctors of death. We, on the other hand, are doctors of life. The elixir allows you life. You'll want to know how it works. You're a doctor, too? Like Ramratan Oak?'

'Microbiologist.'

'Then you'll know. I'll make you a free gift of the idea—in apology to Ramratan Oak.' He patted Ratan's shoulder in farewell. 'Tell the world when you find out.'

Prescott intercepted Ratan at the door. 'Do you know any others?' he asked in an urgent whisper.

Ratan looked at him with contempt.

'Any other hakims?' persisted Prescott. 'He broke the vial! I have just enough for five more years.'

He stayed Ratan with a trembling hand.

'What's five years?' He snapped his fingers. 'Gone, like tomorrow.'

Ratan shook him off and stepped out into the bustle of Colaba Causeway.

Moinuddeen was astride a Bajaj Chetak. Morning light gilded his brown hair. He raised a hand in salute to Ratan.

'It's goodbye to all that now. I'm done with the whole tamasha!'

'What will you do now?'

'What do you think?' The hakim laughed. 'I'll live!'

The Coccyx

'What do you see in the mirror?' Asif Patel's voice was a breathy rasp of complicity.

They were in Asif's clinic. A place more deserted at three in the afternoon would be difficult to imagine. Ratan, in Asif's chair, was wedged between a desk with sharp corners and a sink the size of a soup bowl. A cracked cake of soap, welded to the porcelain, declared the tap a dud. A bottle of hand sanitizer made up for it.

There was a speckled mirror, grotesque in an antique frame. In the mirror, Ratan should have seen Asif lounging in the crumpled scrubs he had sweated in all morning, but Asif's question had rendered him invisible.

Ten minutes ago Ratan had been outed.

Asif's question was about that revelation, but Ratan chose to ignore it. His face frowned back at him resentfully from a perimeter of wrought iron curlicues.

'What do you see in the mirror?' Asif repeated.

'I see myself,' Ratan snapped.

'What do you look like?' persisted Asif.

'Like me!'

'Describe yourself.'

'I'll do nothing of the sort.'

'Wait a moment.'

Asif grabbed the prescription pad and made a few swift passes with a pencil without once raising his eyes from the page.

'Here,' he asked. 'Which one is you?'

Asif had sketched two faces.

Ratan laughed. 'What are you trying to prove? This one is me to the life.'

'Really?' Asif slapped Ratan's wallet down on the table.

'Hey! Where did you get that?'

'Khandani pesha. I come from a long line of pickpockets. Here's your photo ID. Which sketch does this look like?'

After a long silence, Ratan mumbled, 'Nobody looks like their photo ID.'

'Nobody *thinks* they look like their photo ID.'

The second sketch, the one Ratan had spurned, was an exact replica of his photograph.

'That's not me.'

Ratan's rejection was flat and definite. 'What's all this about, anyway?' he demanded as he restored the wallet to his hip pocket.

Asif shrugged. 'You started it. You told me you're two people. I wanted to see your other self.'

'Impossible. How could you possibly know what he looked like?'

'You told me.'

'No, I did not.'

'Not in so many words, but through your gestures. You smooth down an imaginary moustache. I haven't included that in the sketch, but I've shaped the planes of your face in the manner your hand defines them. When deep in thought, you massage your forehead as if it were narrower and more bossed than it really is. Your fingertip often traces your ear meditatively, as if seeking a different curve. This sketch has all these features—and you identified it at once as yourself.'

Ratan was impressed.

In their brief acquaintance of a few months, Asif Patel had not revealed himself as a particularly intelligent man.

As though he read the thought, Asif grinned. 'I told you we were pickpockets, con men, petty thieves. You have to be a good observer to make the grade. I chose a different profession. I was the first in my family to go to college. Of course, it's been two generations since the family turned honest, but if we've kept the law, we've kept our skills too.'

'That explains how you guessed my ...' Ratan's voice trailed off.

Seven years of acknowledging his other life, he didn't yet know what to call it.

'Your other self? I did not guess. You showed it to me, Ratan. It is not as uncommon as you think.'

'What? You know others who have two selves?'

'All of us do, though we don't concede it as openly as you do. I'm Taufiq sometimes. He's the most celebrated thief in our family. Long dead, but lives on as legend. When I'm doing a really tricky bit of surgery, I use Taufiq's fingers, not my own.'

'That's different. That's volitional. He inspires you.'

'Not entirely. All of us brothers, we carry a vestige of Taufiq. Ahmad plays the sitar, and Ismail is a magician. They're both more dextrous than me.'

'Inherent skill, then.'

'No. It doesn't show up all the time. Only under pressure does the vestige assert itself. So, you see, we're not that different from you.'

'Ramratan is hardly a vestige—'

'Nor is the appendix when you have appendicitis. Then it is all of you.'

'I'll go with that. When I'm under pressure, Ramratan confronts me. That's not to say I don't feel the occasional twinge from him when I'm at peace. He might pop up any time. But, he's always relevant to the moment.'

'That's even closer to what I mean. We're always aware of the vestiges we carry. We don't name them, not consciously. Yet, somewhere on the body's map, we know they're there.'

'The body's map? What's that?'

'It is your image of yourself. The Who you see in the mirror. I tell you, Ratan, when I did a stint in plastic surgery, it used to shock me every day. People who had the worst scars and deformities rarely noticed them. The mirror only showed them what they expected to see.'

'A bit philosophical for a guy who works with his hands.'

'Is it? Hand and eye work together.'

'What did your eyes see the last time you used your hands in the theatre?'

Ratan's question stunned Asif Patel into a long silence. Eventually, he narrowed his eyes and began to speak rapidly. 'Funny you should ask that question. I've turned it over in my mind for a week. Funny, too, that we should be talking about vestiges...

* * *

Last Monday, I had a long list. I'd been on my feet for seven hours when I was called out for an emergency. The man on the gurney was very nearly dead. Almost not there. A glass effigy of a man. A sculpture of some cloudy material that might suddenly blaze into brightness like a bulb.

Soon, of course, my fancy was explained clinically.

The man was in shock. Pulseless, cold. He was in pain, this

stony stillness his last defense. The diagnosis was obvious, the abdomen so rigid, it barely moved with each shallow breath.

I had taken in all this when I became aware of his furious stare. For someone a hairsbreadth from death, that was a lot of anger.

The man accompanying him was about our age.

'Your father is very seriously ill,' I began.

'Grandfather,' he interrupted.

That's when I noticed the man's age.

His glassy appearance wasn't just shock, it was the porcelain fragility of extreme age. The taut, almost youthful skin was probably water retention.

As I spoke with the grandson, I puzzled over my anger. For I was suddenly, unaccountably, enraged. What was I angry about? Was I reacting to the fury in the patient's eyes? Or was I reading in them a reflection of my own rage?

No, he *was* angry.

I forced myself to give him the usual anodyne assurances, though in all honesty, there was little I thought I could do. Peritonitis, endotoxic shock, almost to the point of no return.

But he rallied—how quickly he rallied. He stabilized after we had flooded him with a couple of pints. Knowing how brief this window could be, I rushed him to the theatre.

The anesthetist was Desai. You know him. Great guy. I never work with anyone else, if I can avoid it.

I was scrubbed up already when Desai came up to me and said, 'Asif, I'm a bit nervous.'

'You? Impossible. What about?'

'This is my first time.'

And, believe it or not, he blushed, his bat ears like scarlet flags.

'What are you being such a bashful virgin about?

'He is my first centenarian, Asif. I bet you didn't know he's a hundred and five.'

I didn't, but I didn't want to make much of it, either.

'Eighty-five,' I assured Desai, 'not a day more.'

'They have a birth certificate.'

'They'll have a death certificate too if we don't hurry.'

When we got him onto the operating table, the patient still glared at me.

I was beginning to think it was all part of his disordered metabolic state, but—I don't know how better to explain it—his rage seemed so *sane*.

He put out a hand to touch me. I backed away hastily, I was already gowned.

I asked him what he wanted.

'When can I go home?'

'As soon as you're better.'

He gnashed his teeth—he actually did.

I was surprised he had any teeth at all.

Contorted with rage, he was no longer so exquisite.

I felt my own anger return. It upset me.

I moved towards Desai's trolley and was a little surprised when I noticed him setting up for spinal anesthesia.

Really? In a hundred-year-old spine! How would he even get into the intervertebral space?

Desai assured me a continuous epidural would be the safest. 'I've no intention of losing my first hundred-year-old on the table.'

But the patient had other ideas.

When his pyjamas were lowered, we found a complicated langote in place. I barked a bit at that, but the old man's snarl explained why the nurses had baulked at prepping him. He defended that langote like a lion guarding its prey.

We sedated him.

I wondered what peculiarity he was so frantically concealing, when I heard Desai exclaim, and hurried over to his side.

There was a thick scar, a keloid, on the old man's back.

A deep jagged V plunged between his baggy buttocks, the kind of scar you expect if part of the sacrum or the coccyx were excised. Teratomas are common there. The old fellow probably had one removed during childhood.

Teratomas fascinate me, you know. They are twins that quarreled in the womb—one made it, the other wouldn't die outright, and so stuck on...as a tumour.

* * *

'Teratoma? Hah!'

* * *

That wasn't Asif Patel's voice. It was Ramratan's familiar chuckle. Ratan played deaf.

* * *

'So what does this pickpocket know about teratomas?'

* * *

'He's a surgeon,' Ratan responded loftily. He had discovered, of late, that he could sustain a silent conversation with Ramratan—for a while. He never could predict when he would be catapulted into Ramratan's world.

* * *

'Ask him! Was it a teratoma?'

* * *

'Was it a teratoma?' Ratan asked.

Asif Patel looked puzzled.

Ratan tried to clamber back on board. 'So what was it, finally?'

'Burst appendix. Big gaping hole in the cæcum, the appendix had blown off. Found it in a pool of pus in the pelvis. Fæcal peritonitis. I was upto my elbows in muck. Nasty job.'

'But you got him out of it.'

'Nah. He got himself out of it. What a will to live, Ratan! And guess what he does, the first thing, when the sedation wears off—'

* * *

'—he checks on the langote?'

* * *

Ratan was disconcerted to find Asif had heard that.

'Exactly! Luckily Desai had it back in place before he woke up. You should have seen the happy smile when he found it undisturbed. No concern about being still alive. All the fucker cared about was that bloody langote! I showed him the ruptured appendix, and you know what his response was?'

* * *

'I can guess.'

* * *

Ratan shut him up angrily and shook his head.

'He said, "Bah. That's one vestige I can live without." Vestige, Ratan, he said *vestige*!'

'What's surprising about that?'

'I didn't expect him to know that the appendix is a vestigial organ.'

'Why not? For all you know, he's a surgeon himself?'

'No!' Asif's protest was almost a howl of horror.

A long silence ensued and Ratan was loathe to break it.

'I understand now,' Asif said with hesitation. 'I understand what my eyes saw when my hands were at work that day. It wasn't him at all. It was me.'

'What do you mean?'

'As my hands worked hard to keep him alive, I hated what I was doing. I was outraged. I had lost a teenager earlier that week. And now this guy! A hundred and five, perforated appendix, fæcal peritonitis. He had no business being alive! It was unnatural. And yet, I was doing my damnedest to keep him alive. What do you call that, Ratan? Hypocrisy?'

'It is called doing your job. We're all basically indecent—work keeps us decent.'

'You're a cynic.'

'Low down and dirty.'

* * *

'What's his name?'

* * *

His voice startled Ratan into repeating the question.

'Same as mine. Patel. L. K. Patel. Lakulish Kumar Patel.'

Ramratan laughed, the hearty laugh of triumph, not amusement.

* * *

'Laggulish, not Lakulish.'

* * *

Again, Asif heard it.

'You didn't really say that, did you, Ratan?' he asked quietly.

'Lakulish.'

'No. Earlier. It was *him.*'

Ratan shrugged and remained silent. It was impossible to explain. He had already said too much. Time to leave, now.

* * *

'Caught the bugger, at last. Let's go look up Laggulish.'

* * *

Ratan accompanied Asif on his rounds that evening. It just seemed the natural thing to do.

After that conversation, Asif had dozed off on the couch, and Ratan was left to worry about Ramratan's mysterious intrusion. Asif's snoring bulk was oddly reassuring, it anchored Ratan in 1999 as he tried to ignore the headache that was building up its usual ferocity.

At four, Asif called for a syrupy glass of adrak chai, then changed into street clothes.

His transformation was startling. The bland blue shirt changed his face, the skin became taut and shiny, the mouth a neat pleat of politeness, the eyes masked.

L. K. Patel was sitting up in bed, reading.

He greeted Asif with a blank stare.

Asif bent to examine the patient's abdomen.

At the sight of the old man, Ratan felt dizzy.

'You seem to be doing fine without your vestige,' Asif remarked, as he straightened up.

'I did say earlier, the appendix is a vestige I can do without,' the old man responded testily.

* * *

'Ah, just as I suspected. He has it still, the rascal!' said Ramratan.

'I can't believe it,' declared Nusser.

They were watching a young man stride away across Elphinstone Circle.

'How do you know?' demanded Nusser.

'Told me so himself.'

'He showed it to you?'

'We were at a public lecture, Nusser. He was on stage, arguing. He would have won the argument, had he dropped his pants.'

'What was the lecture about?'

'The Missing Link. What else is the Royal Society jawing about these days? It was about Haeckel's Evolutionary Theory.'

'Wasn't that discredited? All those embryos crowding our Anatomy texts were a fraud, weren't they?'

'Those drawings, yes. But Haeckel's idea—'

'Ontogeny recapitulates phylogeny.'

'Yes, we shouldn't discount that. True, carried away by his white skin, Haeckel made an ass of himself.'

'Humanity in ten races, his on the top, and ours right at the bottom.'

'No, you would be in layer six or seven. I would qualify for nine. I've met him, did you know that?'

'Who, Haeckel? When were you ever in Jena?'

'Right here, in Bombay.'

'How did I miss that?'

'Let me see—'81.'

'I was in England.'

'I had forgotten all about it until this afternoon, when I saw this chap. A spitting image of his grandfather, or I wouldn't have remembered Haeckel at all.'

* * *

'You're the spitting image of your grandfather, or, I wouldn't have remembered Haeckel at all,' said Ratan.

In the hiatus that followed, his voice reverberated, loud and foolish. He cursed inwardly, but it was too late for a retraction.

The old man's eyes narrowed to brilliant slits.

Ratan felt ice in his veins. Everything in him turned cold, tight, compacted for a fight. What was this quarrel about?

'You know of my grandfather? He's scarcely remembered these days. Where did you hear of him?'

'His life was—interesting.' Now why did he say that?

'He made a lot of money, if that's what you mean. Today he would be a billionaire. Yes, they say I do resemble him. There are a few portraits. We have one at home. It is home no longer. My son has turned it into a hotel. The Chhaya Grand. Named it after his mother—she was a princess. Her father was a minor raja, I forget where. You saw the portrait in the hotel?'

'At Darukavana, yes.'

'You know the old name? Darukhana we used to call it. Do you know why it was called Darukavana?'

* * *

'Do you know why it's called Darukavana?' the guest asked.

Ramratan was halfway up the stairs when the question hit him like a slingshot. As yet, the guest had no name.

Ramratan had entered the house minutes ago to find his father deep in conversation with a visitor.

The brief glimpse suggested richness, even magnificence. The sheen of his silk djibba, the flow of his muslin panchakaccha, the brilliance of his ear studs, all bespoke a maharajah, at the very least. Or else an actor from the Play House.

Krishnaji Oak, catching sight of his son, called out to him, and Ramratan was forced to make a polite greeting.

No actor, this one. He was a genuine grandee.

A tall man in his early fifties, he had a singularly beautiful face. His features were not symmetrical, but they shone with a radiance difficult to ignore.

'So this is your son,' the man murmured as Ramratan made his pranam.

'Patel Saheb lives in Darukavana,' explained Krishnaji.

'Oh!' Ramratan, about to excuse himself, paused.

Patel Saheb smiled. 'Your father tells me you find the house fascinating. I'll be happy to show you around any time you care to visit.'

Ramratan thanked him, and pleading an exam next morning, made his retreat. He was halfway up the stairs when Patel Saheb's question arrested him. 'Do you know why it's called Darukavana?'

'No. That's what fascinated me,' Ramratan admitted. 'Cedars in Bombay? Do they grow in your garden?'

'Mohsin Ahmad warned me that would be your first question. Please come back, Ramratan.' The voice was a gentle command, but the man's eyes were pleading.

'I know you have an exam tomorrow, and surgical anatomy is one of your subjects. Don't be surprised, Vandyke Carter is a dear friend of mine.'

'Professor Carter is safe in England,' Ramratan laughed.

'Well, I've heard him mention you as his star pupil. Vandyke Carter is in the city presently, but this is not a matter I wish to discuss with him. Frankly, I've sought you out as a refuge from my old friend. The fact is, Ramratan, I need a doctor—or an anatomist, and Mohsin recommended you. Tell me, Ramratan, what do you think of Darwin's ideas?'

'The Origin is the most fascinating book I've ever read.'

'Good, that makes this easier. Have you heard of Ernst Haeckel?'

'What, the polygenist?'

'Bravo! Yes, indeed. Ernst Haeckel argues that humanity has different origins. Ten races, according to him, arranged hierarchically.'

'Obviously, the white man heads the list.'

'Obviously. But it is not entirely a white man's idea. We were a stratified society long before the white man ever looked our way. So, you do know Haeckel. Have you, perhaps, also heard about his idea of the Missing Link?'

'Half chimp, half human? He can't be serious.'

'He is, I assure you, and he is here, looking for it.'

'Here? In Bombay?'

'Indeed.'

'Do you think he'll find the Missing Link here?'

'Specifically, in Darukavana.'

'In your house?'

'The wanderer of Darukavana, do you know him?'

Ramratan tried to recall the legend, but it was a mixed-up memory.

'Shiva?' He ventured.

'Yes. Shiva as Lakulisha. You know the word.'

'No. I don't know Sanskrit.'

'Lakulisha is the lord with the club or staff. Aha, I see the coin has dropped.'

Ramratan recollected the figure of Lakulisha from cave sculptures—a hearty young man with a gigantic erection, calmly ignoring a bevy of admiring damsels.

'I see you have rightly concluded the club or staff to be a necessary euphemism. Lakulisha wandered the forest of cedars tormented and priapic. Cursed by the rishis, he lost his phallus. That's the story. Now, what if he were not Lakulisha but Laggulish?'

'Ah.' Krishnaji drew a deep breath.

Ramratan shook his head, mystified.

'The boy does not understand. Forgive me—' Krishnaji's words ended in a sound of alarm. Father and son stared at the visitor, unable to look away.

Patel Saheb's pancha of fine silk had slid off him like a shimmering snakeskin.

The langote went the way of the dhoti, and Patel Saheb whirled around, displaying his back.

If they had been astonished earlier, they were now petrified with amazement.

Pendant between Patel Saheb's lordly buttocks was a thick recurvate tail.

It was covered by a dense mat of shiny black bristles.

As they watched, the tail rose a few inches and essayed a feeble wag. Krishnaji, overcome, clutched Ramratan's shoulder for support.

'Please feel free to examine it.' Patel Saheb's calm voice penetrated the fog. Krishnaji nodded uncertainly.

Ramratan was horrified by his own horror. Had he seen this in the Out Patients he would have plunged joyously into discovery, eager to refute all he had read with his own observations. But here, at home, it was very different. Here the body was nudity, the world's image of itself. Disconnected from the physical reality of skin, muscle, bone, it had become pudic, ludic, ridic. A shocking ornament, a salacious tease. Offense.

He heard himself say, 'Yes, I will. I'd like you to keep standing, but do let me know if you'd prefer to sit.'

'No, I'm perfectly comfortable. Please go ahead, Doctor.'

* * *

Ramratan touched the tail, and was faintly surprised when it felt warm and firm. Despite the fur, he had expected something cold, scaly, prehensile.

There was a smooth continuity in the curve of the spine and that of the tail. The votive meander of the sacrum funneled down to segments of the coccyx or tail bone.

True tails, he recalled, never contained vertebrae—yet surely, that is what his fingers palpated. In continuity with the four coccygeal segments, small hard fragments were beaded all the way to the tip.

There was a second contradiction: this was no inanimate vestige. The tail had responded to his touch with a shudder of horripilation. A rush of something sweet and corrupt tainted the air.

He realized, with dismay, that the tail had a scent gland positioned very much like a dog's. He should have noticed the tiny island devoid of hair, a common sight on any randy dog.

His distress increased when he noticed the fine sheen of sweat which now bedewed the buttocks.

'Thank you, please resume your clothing now,' he managed to say and rushed out to wash his hands.

When he returned, Patel Saheb, clothes and tranquility restored, was seated magisterially in the armchair.

Paradoxically, it detracted from his grandeur. His pale skin and flowing pancha gave him the mortuary air of Victorian statuary.

Ramratan met the man's calm look of enquiry and said, 'It is an atavism. Not unknown, though I've never seen one before.'

'Atavism. Vestige. Persistence of an ancestral trait. Yes, I know all those labels. I need more than that, Ramratan. Am I the Missing Link?'

'No, sir. I don't think you could make that claim. I do know a bit about tails in humans, and this is just an accidental aberration.'

'Aberration. Yes, I left out that one. Look, son, I have crossed fifty years with that concealed in my langote, but the matter is not that simple. There is a belief—no proof, mind you, just a belief—that it recurs in the family. I'm from Karvan, if you must know, the original site of Lakulisha. Laggulisha it must have been all along, *Laggula* is tail, as you father will affirm. Last week, I had my first grandchild. A boy, thank God. Such a life inflicted on a woman would be unthinkable. Yes, Ramratan, a boy born with a tail like mine. Another Laggulish.'

Ramratan was about to say the child need not suffer. An excision was a simple surgical procedure. His friend Salim—

As if he read the thought, Patel Saheb raised a cautionary finger. 'Do not, I beg of you, speak of excision, amputation, removal, or whatever the present euphemism is. I will not allow such mutilation. It will endanger the child's life.'

'That is your decision entirely.' Ramratan shrugged. 'But I must tell you the surgery isn't risky.'

'You misunderstand me. It is not the procedure that will endanger his life. Without his tail, that child will die.'

'I disagree. It is just a vestige. It has no purpose, no

function whatsoever. He won't even know he had a tail. Have you not wanted to be rid of yours?'

'That is an impertinence I will ignore, and pass on to my request. I would like you to be present on Sunday afternoon when I show the baby to Ernst Haeckel. I wish to hear his opinion. Does this tail place us in a different category of human beings? Can our difference, in some manner, illuminate and further an understanding of our origins? It is a duty I owe science. We founder, Ramratan, in a morass of ignorance, and the only purpose of life is to free ourselves of its mire. There is that lotus in us all, don't you agree?'

Ramratan felt his eyes burn with unexpected tears. Whether shame or pain provoked them, he could not tell.

* * *

Sunday, 13 November, 1881

Ernst Haeckel was the guest of Herr Blaschek, a German businessman, lodged luxuriously on Malabar Hill.

Ramratan's visits to the Hill were rare. When he accompanied one of his Professors on a private visit, his role was distressingly ambiguous. More than once he had been requested to wait in the verandah lest his native breath pollute the sick room. When assisting at minor surgery, his presence was endured, but he was certain they counted the spoons the moment his back was turned.

The Villa Blaschek received them with more grace. Largely, Ramratan suspected, because gifts from Darukavana had preceded them.

The baby, nestled preciously in its many wrappings, had slept peacefully through the ride in the grandfather's arms.

Patel Saheb's letter of introduction was inscribed with a coat of arms. His liveried footman proffered it on a salver of gold.

They were admitted immediately. Herr Blaschek himself hurried out to welcome them.

Ernst Haeckel was a few years younger than Patel Saheb, a stocky man with a red beard and pale grey eyes. This contrast in his colouring, and the anarchy of his luxuriant hair, gave him the look of a seer at the very precipice of prophecy. He greeted them a few complimentary sentiments that Patel Saheb reciprocated with grace.

The baby slept on unperturbed, his presence acknowledged only by Frau Blaschek who made kind enquiries after the mother.

Haeckel admitted to three children, and was warmly congratulated on the achievement.

Eventually, Haeckel arrived at the letter. It lay open on the desk before them.

'This says you would like my opinion on a scientific matter,' he began delicately. 'It alludes to the infant?'

'Yes.'

Haeckel said something in German and, unwillingly, Frau Blaschek left the room. Her husband was about to follow when Patel Saheb restrained him.

Ramratan wondered if the baby had been fed a convenient dose of Balamrut, the popular opiate. But as the wrappings fell away, it woke up, and gurgled and kicked in happy abandon.

Haeckel, quite enchanted, held out a finger which the baby sucked obligingly.

Patel Saheb picked the baby up tenderly and laid him down on his stomach.

Haeckel erupted in an excited flood of German, then recollected himself, and said, 'This is indeed unusual!'

'It is a tail,' Patel Saheb stated.

And, he omitted to add, a miniature replica of his own.

Haeckel asked no questions at all. He examined the baby carefully, then made a few rapid sketches in his notebook.

'What is the significance of this tail, Herr Haeckel?' Patel Saheb asked. 'Does it have some relevance to the Missing Link?'

'Indeed, it appears so,' replied Haeckel thoughtfully.

'What do you expect—foresee—in the development of this child?'

'It is hard to say, and difficult to predict,' mused Haeckel. Then he spoke earnestly in German to Herr Blaschek, who seemed a little taken aback, but nodded gravely just the same.

To Ramratan's surprise, Patel Saheb answered Haeckel in German. The words were unintelligible, but his anger was obvious.

'Do not think, not for a moment, that I will permit you to make a Hottentot Venus of this child!' he concluded in English. 'I'm sorry I have wasted your time. Herr Blaschek, my thanks to you and your gracious wife for your courtesy in receiving me.'

Picking up the baby and disdaining Haeckel's outstretched hand, he marched out in high dudgeon.

The story of the Hottentot Venus was common knowledge. European savants had usurped the life of Saartjie Baartman, a young woman of the Khoi-Khoi tribe from the Gamtoos River Valley in the Cape of Good Hope. She had died caged like an animal. In the forced exile from her homeland, she suffered every possible indignity a woman can imagine. Her humiliations did not end with death. Ramratan knew a man who had paid good money in a Paris Museum to gawk at her genitals pickled in formalin.

No words were spoken on the way back, though the baby howled his lungs out.

At the foot of the Ghodapdeo Hill, Ramratan was let go, with a cold word of thanks.

He stormed into the house, furious and humiliated almost as much as Saartjie Baartman.

Later that week a letter arrived with a box of books.

Ramratan retained the letter, unopened. The books he sent back with a curt note: *Your kindness is appreciated, but unacceptable.*

He said nothing of this to his father.

A month later, Mohsin Chacha suggested, 'I think it is time you opened that letter.'

Resentfully, Ramratan let another month slip by before he finally opened Patel Saheb's letter.

It was an apology, ending with the words:

> *Perhaps you will find it in your heart to forgive my rudeness, and consider my plea. In future, should my grandson ever need your help, I beg of you not to refuse it.*

Ramaratan ran all the way to Darukavana, but Patel Saheb was no longer there. Nothing was to be got out of Mohsin either. The strange man and his caudate grandson had vanished as if they had never been.

Ramratan read of Haeckel often, and always with loathing.

* * *

Wednesday, 10 October, 1906

Ramratan attended the lecture at the Asiatic at Yashoda's prodding. He was all for getting back to the case that bothered him, but that wouldn't do for her, would it? As usual, she refused to accompany him.

'I can't read the world for you, Yashoda,' he protested for the millionth time.

'You're my spectacles.'

The title of the lecture: *The Germ Plasm Theory and Inheritance*, meant little to him. But as the speaker began, it all came flooding back.

Weismann's experiment that proved acquired traits were not heritable—68 mice with their tails amputated went on to produce generations with tails. Weismann's triumphant statement returned to memory: *901 young were produced by five generations of artificially mutilated parents, and yet there was not a single example of a rudimentary tail or of any other abnormality in this organ—*

Ramratan gnashed his teeth. Why was something so self-evident being passed off as science?

And then, before questions could be invited, a young man sprang up and harangued the Chair, demanding to be heard.

The Chair tried to shut him up, but the fellow was having none of that. He bounded up to the dais.

'Weissman's experiments have no meaning!' he shouted. 'Why bother about the next generation? What were his observations on the mice whose tails he cut off? How did their behaviour change?'

The bewildered speaker tried, in vain, to make himself heard.

Nothing could silence his questioner.

In a desperate move to end the fracas, refreshments were announced half an hour early, and led to a general stampede.

The young man was left pacing the dais angrily.

It was then that Ramratan noticed his face—and Lakulish Kant Patel of Darukavana leapt in memory. Here was the young and modern version—surely the caudate grandchild he had accompanied to the Villa Blaschek.

Ramratan calculated rapidly—the boy must be what, twenty-seven? Absurdly young.

'Laggulish Patel.'

The young man stopped pacing. In the stillness, his voice was barely above a whisper. 'Did you say— Laggulish?'

'Lakulish.'

'No. You did say Laggulish.'

Ramratan shrugged. 'Yes, I did. I knew Patel Saheb, your grandfather. Perhaps this evening, I alone understood the weight of your argument.'

Lakulish stepped down from the dais, but made no attempt to approach Ramratan. They stared at each other across the maze of chairs.

How like mice we are, thought Ramratan, quivering before we approach the moment.

'You must be him,' the boy said at last. 'Quercus indica, my grandfather called you. He told me I should find you one day, and look, you have found me, Dr Oak.'

'I'm glad. I respected your grandfather.'

'He brought me up. He died when I was twenty. Listen, I'd like to meet you again. Can I come to your office? Consulting rooms?'

'You can come home.'

'No. Perhaps later. Please?'

'Yes, of course. Any Thursday afternoon.' Ramaratan gave him the address.

'I—I'd like to explain my outburst. I didn't mean to cause a disturbance. I just wanted to know.'

'I understand.'

'What did those mice feel when their tails were cut off? How did they perceive it? Mutilation? Deprivation? How did it change their lives? Where is the tail in the map?'

'Map?'

'In the body's map? In your map of yourself, Dr Oak. Shut your eyes for a moment. Humour me, please. Shut your eyes and look at yourself. What do you see?'

Ramratan saw nothing, though the boy's earnestness compelled a sincere effort. He admitted as much.

'That's because you're ordinary. When you're extraordinary, like me, the extra bit is all you see.'

'You see your tail?'

'No. I see the meaning of my tail. I see—Ubermensch.'

Nietzsche. What next? He had been a little hasty about Thursday afternoon.

'This Thursday, then? Four o'clock. Excellent. I'll see you then.'

And he was gone.

After this encounter, Ramratan found Nusser's calm sanity a relief. He found himself blurting out Lakulish's secret.

Nusser, dependably phlegmatic, was unimpressed.

The talk returned to Ramratan's worrying case.

'The press is enjoying it,' said Nusser. 'The *Times*—'

'—calls him the Bombay Ripper,' Ramratan growled.

'Hardly an exaggeration.'

'Well, he doesn't kill them.'

'Just leaves them for dead.'

Nusser was right. This young woman of twenty had died yesterday. She was the fourth case in six months.

'What do you think, Ramratan? Edwardes is depending on you.'

If he landed the Bombay Ripper, it would mean a Kaiser-i-Hind, at the very least, for Police Commissioner S. M. Edwardes. As Police Surgeon, Ramratan Oak was still graded 'Native Assistant.'

Still, Edwardes was a good man, and Ramratan wished he had something more to give him other than the vague picture he had formulated of the Bombay Ripper (darn, the name had stuck!).

The Ripper ambushed his victims in secluded spaces within crowds—in stairwells, in pillared arcades, beneath bridges.

How did he rape and mutilate so swiftly, and so covertly, in broad daylight? That alone made Ramratan certain the Ripper was a tall and powerfully built fellow.

Paradoxically, evidence at the crime scene— the spatter of blood and semen—suggested the uncontrollable frenzy of insanity. Such criminals were usually small insignificant-looking men.

All the victims had been blindfolded and gagged. None of them had seen the assailant.

'I'm totally in the dark,' Ramratan confessed. 'He could be just about anybody.'

'Insane, you think?'

'Indubitably.' Ramratan wished he were as certain as he sounded.

'Maybe Edwardes should look into the Asylums.' Nusser's lame suggestion concluded the conversation.

Ramratan walked home morose and despairing, crushed by his responsibility and ignorance. He had never felt so utterly powerless.

Unlike Nusser, he did not think the elusive Ripper was a lunatic at large. He was probably a respectable man, leading a life of cloying domesticity.

Ramratan, at fifty-one, thought himself an expert on

the dead. What did he understand of life if he couldn't read his fellow men? And that boy—that mere stripling who hadn't crossed the threshold into manhood, that— that monkey—he thought of himself as Ubermensch?

Still, the boy had an intelligent mind.

The seer of the body, the philosophic Self, consciousness, the first step into tát túvam ási—the boy had got that far. Patel Saheb's tutelage had paid off.

Darukavana, the place of enlightenment.

* * *

'Darukavana, the place of enlightenment,' said Ratan.

'And you know why.'

'Yes.' Ratan was terse.

'You're a wise fellow! What do they call you?'

'*Quercus indica.*' The words were out before he could stop them.

The old man's eyes widened—almost with terror. Then a sardonic smile twisted his lips.

'Of course. You have a grandfather too. Or great-grandfather?'

'Yes.'

'Dr Oak.'

'That is my name, yes.'

'So what did the senior Dr Oak tell you about me?'

* * *

'Say nothing.'

* * *

Ratan shrugged.

The old man mirrored Ratan's gesture. 'At my age, this muscular movement is painful. I want to conserve my

energies for the muscles that matter, I can't afford to shrug
and prevaricate. What the hell, you know it already. Dr Patel,
you saw the scar on my back. What did you think it was?

'Yes, I did. It was curious. A sacral tumour?'

'A teratoma? An aborted twin? No. This is an amputation
scar. Self-inflicted.'

'Impossible,' Asif protested.

'Oh, I didn't do the operation, it was done at my behest.'

'Ubermensch,' said Ratan with scorn.

'Yes, that's what I was. What I couldn't face up to. And
you're the reason for that, Dr Oak! How close you came to
destroying my life. You never guessed, did you?'

Ratan shook his head. Ramratan, in his skull, held his
breath, all energy concentrated on the old man.

'My grandfather was the motive force. Dr Oak was merely
a willing accessory. The first time—actually, the second time
he saw me—'

* * *

Ramratan had forgotten all about Laggulish when he
turned up the following Thursday. By then, the Ripper,
as he was now commonly called, had claimed another
victim.

She too had succumbed to her horrific injuries.

Ramratan, heartsick, had just concluded his autopsy
report when Laggulish strolled in without as much as a
knock.

The sight of him infuriated Ramratan. He scowled,
but remained silent. The hair on his nape bristled.
This atavistic response appropriate to the caecilian
intrusion, restored his humour.

Laggulish took a chair and looked about the small
room with curiosity. 'Not much of an office, is it?'

'It is all I need.'

'You see things immediately, don't you? That's the difference between you and me. Your needs are modest. Mine, immeasurable.'

'If you can meet them, no harm in that.'

'That's refreshing. I was raised by my grandfather. He taught me quite the reverse. Take what you need only if it does no harm. I appoint you as my guru forthwith!'

'Thank you. I have no use for a student.'

'A student like me, you mean?'

'No. Any student. I don't teach—I'm too busy learning.'

'Then let me advance your education.' Lagullish sprang up, shut and bolted the door. And, quite like his venerable grandfather had done, lowered his trousers.

Later, Ramratan would marvel at how much the absence of a langote enhanced the drama. Unrestrained, the tail was a whiplash of brilliance and scent as it shot free with a hot little hiss. The black gloss of its bristles was as iridescent as a pigeon's neck. It left a feral spoor downwind, faintly putrescent, like some venomous flower.

Ramratan was startled by its size. It was as thick as his hand.

'Surprised?' Laggulish grinned.

'Not in the least. I've seen it before.'

'So you tell me. How big was it then?'

'Commensurate with your size. You were a week old.'

'I had to conceal it until I was a teenager, did you know that? It became sheer torture, even Grandfather took pity on me.'

'Part of the growth spurt.'

'How wise you think you are, Dr Oak. What do you know about it?'

'You're right. Tell me. Why did it torment you?'

'It drove me wild. I was—uncontrollable.'

'Did you feel better after it was—er, freed?'

'Yes. After dark I was allowed to roam about Darukavana with it exposed. I started to yearn for the sun on it, so I was let loose on the terrace. That's when Grandfather caught me with the gardener's daughter. After that it was back to jail again.'

'Must have been hard to bear. '

'You can't imagine. But Grandfather could. You see, he had suffered in the same manner.'

'Then his advice would have been practical.'

'If I had his mind, yes. I think of him with great reverence, don't mistake me, but he was not the man I am.'

'Which is?'

'Ubermensch.'

Ramratan laughed.

Laggulish's face fell. He packed up his tail, curled it carefully before he pulled up his pants.

'I see you don't believe me,' he said sadly. 'No matter. The tail compels me to greatness.'

'As long as you do no harm.'

'To myself? No, I won't.'

Ramratan recognized the futility of argument and let the fellow go.

There were four more attacks by the Ripper that year, and Ramratan had neither time nor inclination for distractions of any sort. He had failed dismally to pin down any dependable piece of evidence.

There was panic on the Hill as a memsahib reported an attack. After questioning her, Ramratan was unconvinced. A rough lover, probably picked from 'the menials' for an afternoon or two, was his diagnosis.

And then it all ceased.

For four months, there was peace.

It was during this hiatus that Laggulish turned up again.

A very different man entered this time. Gone was the gay blade with his Byronic fire. This man was morose, almost withdrawn. He avoided Ramratan's eyes even as he sought him out.

'I'm in something of a crisis. Grandfather told me to take your advice if I was ever in trouble, and I am now.'

'Why, what's the matter?'

'They want to get me married.'

'Your parents?'

'Yes. They hardly know me. They've never lived at Darukavana. They've never even seen it.'

'The house?'

'No! My tail.'

'Impossible.'

'Not really. Grandfather had this caretaker couple raise me. I had no relationship with them. They were useful, though. After the man died, his wife tried to blackmail me, so I got rid of her.'

'Paid her?'

'Not a chance. I got rid of her.'

'Well?'

'Now my parents are back, and they want me married.'

'What do you want Laggulish?'

'An ordinary life. I'm tired.'

'Tired of being Ubermensch?'

'No, that won't change. I'm just tired of the other thing.'

'The tail.'

'Of its compulsions, yes.'

'Chop it off, then.'

'How callous you are.'

'Not at all. That was my advice to your grandfather too when I first saw you.'

'What did he say?'

Ramratan hesitated. Then, with deliberation, he lied. 'He was afraid of the risks of surgery.'

'What are the risks?'

'No more than those for any minor surgery. It is a trivial procedure, really.'

'He told me I should have surgery if it ever became unbearable. He anticipated this moment. Once I decided about it, he suggested I should seek you out. Here I am. Do what you will, but rid me of this horror. It will have to be done secretly. Can you—'

'Yes, that can be managed.'

A great weight seemed to lift off Laggulish. His face assumed the radiance Ramratan had so admired in Patel Saheb.

He clasped Ramratan's hands in a steely grip. 'How can I ever repay you?'

'Will you pay me what I ask?'

'Twice over. I'm a rich man, Dr Oak.'

'Twice over won't be necessary. I want the resected specimen for my Museum. Will you give it to me? I will dissect and study it.'

'Of course. I just want to be rid of it.'

And so it was done.

* * *

'And so it was done,' the old man said.

'The surgery?' Asif was solicitous, intent on detail.

'Yes, yes, what else? And he took it from me, your grandfather—'

'The specimen,' Asif interrupted, 'the teratoma?'

'Call it that, if you will. Yes! He took it without a thought!' Rage suffused the old man's face.

'You gave it to him,' Ratan countered.

'He should have known what would happen to me!' He struck the bed violently. 'Go! Get out of my sight!'

Ratan stepped out, his heart pounding more from Ramratan's distress than his own.

He found his bike, and raced through the congested Muhammad Ali Road.

He was just in time.

Bhimashankar was preparing to lock up the Museum, but he grinned knowingly when he saw Ratan and sent out for chai. The staff indulged Ratan's after-hours in the little room on the mezzanine.

He had wangled this space from Crispin to house Ramratan's treasures. He had discovered them relegated to the basement as junk. Specimens, files, a steel cupboard, and a certain tin trunk, as yet unopened.

Ratan meant to catalogue them all one day. For now they stayed, grimy and cobwebbed. There were more than 500 specimen jars—how was he to find the one he wanted? Ramratan remained stubbornly silent.

Oh well. He would start with the registers.

Ratan yanked open the cupboard.

Here at least was order.

He had been the first to open the cupboard in 1992, fifty-two years after Ramratan had locked it for the final time.

He opened the register for 1906 when he heard Ramratan make an impatient sound.

Of course—*1907.*

Half an hour later, he found what he was looking for.

Human tail, dissection; R. Oak; April 25, 1907. Number 352/250407. *

* * *

'Incredible. I couldn't believe what I was seeing.'

Ramratan couldn't believe his eyes. He had begun dissecting Laggulish's appendage an hour ago. He had expected vestigial bone. He found, instead, six robust vertebrae with strong strappy muscles. Even more disconcerting was the fringe of emerging nerves, too thick and too many to be dismissed as 'normal'.

What was a 'normal tail' in a human being?

Ramaratan completed the dissection with a sense of dread. He waited for the week to run its course, expecting every day a call or a note from Laggulish. He heard nothing.

Two weeks after the surgeon had discharged Laggulish, Ramratan made his way to Darukavana. The gate was locked and barred. The family was not in residence.

More than a little irritated, Ramratan put away Jar Number 352/250407, and with it, the memory of its origin.

The matter did not end there.

Nusser, of all people, brought news about six months later. Laggulish had married the daughter of some minor Raja, and now there was a great scandal because the girl had been sent back to her parents.

'Her parents concluded the usual,' said Nusser. 'That the girl wouldn't do her duty, as they put it. They bullied her and made her miserable, and then the truth came out. She was willing enough. He wasn't. Evidently, your Ubermensch is above carnal appetites.'

'Who could have guessed?' said Ramratan. 'I have

his tail. It is dissected to a marvel. The boy is a boor, and that girl is well rid of him.'

He had the tail—but not for long.

That September the Museum was vandalized.

The break-in was freakishly purposeless. Specimen jars smashed in fury, the floor awash with glass shards, formalin and human debris. Many of the objects on display were missing. Jar Number 352/250407 was among them.

Ramratan had no time to mourn his missing treasures. The Bombay Ripper was back. This time Ramratan was leaving nothing to chance.

The latest victim was a woman of thirty-five, her body mangled beyond belief. She had been attacked at midday, outside Byculla Railway Station. She had defensive cuts on both arms. Her right fist was clenched in cadaveric spasm. She had fought her assailant to the very end.

Had she captured something of him too?

Ramratan eased open her clenched fist. She had grabbed her assailant by the hair. Six glossy black hairs were stuck in her calloused palm. The microscope told him little beyond his initial assessment: the hair had been forcibly pulled out, probably from the head of a young man.

A grim desolation overtook him.

He put away the microscope and was about to lock the room when all his senses flared up in vigilance. His muscles tensed in readiness for the predator's spring.

Through his long acquaintance with violent crime, Ramratan had experienced this too often to discredit the instinct. The Ripper was here. Right here, somewhere very close to him.

Ramratan stayed where he was, effacing himself in

the dark room. He held his breath, but heard no other breathing. Just the same, Ramratan could sense the Ripper, could smell him.

The odour intensified.

Darkness and silence had gagged two senses, the third grew more perspicacious.

A peculiar redolence, ketotic, ammoniacal, apple drenched in stale urine.

Strangely, it seemed to emanate from his desk.

Ramratan froze in horror as he recognized the source.

That hair!

The six hairs in the dead woman's grasp had been torn, not from the Ripper's head, but from his tail.

Ramratan hurried out and walked rapidly towards Darukavana. If the house was locked, he would speak to Edwardes tomorrow—but for now, he would confront the devil himself, and make a citizen's arrest.

The gate was locked, the house beyond was indistinct in the dark.

He did not tell Edwardes, not immediately.

When he did, he merely identified Lakulish Patel as a man who might, in some way, lead them to the Ripper.

Edwardes obligingly put out the word, but Laggulish had disappeared.

* * *

Exhausted by the intensity of recall, Ratan had been staring at Ramratan's entry in the register.

Human tail, dissection; R. Oak; April 25, 1907. Number 352/250407.*

Why had Ramratan stopped looking for Laggulish? What had distracted him?

The answer was evident. The attacks had stopped.

Yet, Ramratan hadn't closed the file. He would surely have referenced the rest of the tale.

Ah. That asterisk. There must be a footnote.

Ramratan had the infuriating habit of writing his footnotes at the end of a list and not at the bottom of each page.

Here it was.

The notation meant it was a specimen. Ratan located it without much difficulty.

A glassine envelope containing six black hairs.

* * *

'Use them! You have all sorts of new tests now. Do them!'

* * *

Asif called that night. 'All okay, Ratan?'

'Yes. What about the old man?'

'Oh, he recovered after you left. Took a dislike to you, definitely. You think he really knew your grandfather?'

'Great-grandfather. Yes.'

'He's certainly kept up the grudge. Anyway, he was asleep when I looked in on him an hour later, fast asleep. By the way, I have something to show you.' He promised to meet Ratan before he started work tomorrow.

Ratan, on the verge of telling him about the Ripper, held his tongue.

Asif looked very happy next morning, like a schoolboy on the first day of vacation.

'That old guy spooked you, didn't he?' Asif grinned. 'I've got a gift for you.'

'He sent me a gift?'

'Not exactly. He got himself into such a state, I thought we'd lose him. He gasped out a request. I could barely understand him. He wanted an object from the bedside table. I gave it to him. A piece of wood, wrapped in silk. He clutched it frantically, and from that moment on, he began to revive. I asked him if it was a talisman, something blessed. He laughed out devilishly and said I could call it so, if I wished. "A piece of the True Cross" if you like. And then, Ratan, he leered so wolfishly at me, I actually felt menaced. That decided me. I returned an hour later, and he was asleep, with that thing still clutched against his chest. Here it is.'

'You—'

'Sure. Easy peasy, done in a blink.'

'What about the hell he'll raise when he wakes up?'

'Really, Ratan! You're asking that of Taufiq?'

'Who's Tauf—oh yes, your light-fingered ancestor.'

'We're all light-fingered, but to do a Taufiq, ah, it makes the heart sing! He's sleeping peacefully holding close a twig wrapped in silk. May it guard him well! Another piece of the True Cross.'

Asif handed Ratan an envelope. 'Keep it or throw it. I just had to get it for you.'

* * *

'It is smaller, much smaller than it used to be. I hadn't allowed for so much shrinkage. Of course, mummification has obscured everything—'

* * *

Mummification?

Ratan ran a cautious fingertip over the twig. Did he imagine it, or were these bristles?

'It is not a twig, Asif,' he said.

* * *

'You can match the hairs now. Comparative microscopy will establish the hairs in the envelope came from this. Don't waste time, Ratan, confront him.'

* * *

'What is it? I'm waiting, Ratan—'

'Asif, I must see him. Now. Before it's too late.'

'Too late for what?'

'I don't know. Asif, I must see him.'

'What's this about, Ratan?'

Ratan showed him the hair in the glassine envelope. 'These once grew on this stick, Asif. They're evidence from a crime scene.'

'They grew on this? Ratan, is this his vestige? The one he can't do without? His—his—'

'Tail. Yes.'

Asif examined the desiccated twig. 'How did I miss this, Ratan? Bristles, definitely. Should have fallen off by now. How long ago was it removed, do you know?'

'April 1907. Stolen from the Museum that September.'

'And you—you remembered all that? *He* told you? Ramratan?'

'Yes.'

Asif's face darkened. 'He didn't fail you, Ratan. Taufiq failed me. My fingers did not feel the bristles. I thought this was cinnamon—you know the stuff? Stinks like hell.'

'Taufiq didn't fail you if you could smell that, Asif.'

* * *

'The supra-caudal gland, tell him Ratan. Dogs have it, hasn't he noticed?'

* * *

'Secretions from the supra-caudal, the violet gland,' Ratan repeated, feeling foolish. 'I can smell nothing, Asif. If you could, that was Taufiq.'

* * *

'Surprising how much comfort a small lie can bring. Go, now, Ratan, time's running out.'

* * *

'Let's go, Asif.'

'You said crime, Ratan. Surely you don't think he's a criminal?'

'Let's find out.'

They were too late.

Ratan cursed himself as they entered the surgical ward.

The place wore the desolate hush that follows a death. Nurses swarmed the counter in a buzz of suppressed excitement. Death is a voyeurism very few can resist.

As they sighted Asif, the girls dispersed.

The Staff Nurse walked with purpose towards him.

Asif hurried forward to meet her. Their conversation concluded, the nurse swept away with a disdainful look at Ratan.

Asif's news relieved Ratan.

Lakulish Patel was very much alive, but after his upset last night, the fight had gone out of the old man. His relatives now expected him to die.

The responsible grandson had turned up at 6 a.m., demanded the bill, paid up in cash—with a handsome extra—and walked out, abandoning the patient. The handsome extra would pay for a pauper's funeral.

Of course, the nurses had kept all this from the old man.

Predictably, he was now a cherished pet. He had just finished breakfast. The nurse particularly requested Asif not to let his friend upset the old man again.

Laggulish was sitting up, reading the paper. Ratan noticed a small silk drawstring bag by his side, presumably containing his relic.

'Dr Oak!' He greeted Ratan with a tremulous smile. 'So good of you to come.'

His hand groped among the bedclothes and closed around the silk bag. His eyes flashed briefly as he opened it and held Asif's twig out to Ratan. 'Do you recognize this?'

Ratan placed the twig on the table and laid his glassine envelope next to it. 'I think they belong together,' he said quietly.

'Hair?' Laggulish frowned, as if trying to capture an elusive memory.

'From the Bombay Ripper.'

'Bombay Ripper?' The old man repeated the words thoughtfully. 'Did they really call me that?'

He leaned forward with a surprising vigour. He grabbed the twig, pressed it against his chest, and glared at Ratan with his old malevolence.

'You knew?'

'Yes, I knew.'

'But you couldn't catch me.'

'I have now.'

'Hah. Who will believe you? Those hairs mean nothing now. They meant a lot to me then.' His voice rose. 'She tore out a whole tuft, the bitch! She hurt me! *Me!*' He struck at the bed with flailing hands.

* * *

'For heaven's sake don't let him get hold of the hair.'

* * *

Laggulish rolled the twig against his chest repeatedly, forcing himself to calm down. 'You can't prove a thing,' he said in a steady voice.

'Yes, I can. I can establish that these hairs belonged—'

'In this?' The old man's fist had closed on his twig. 'Only death will part me from this. I'm immortal, you hear? Immortal!'

'I won't attempt to take that from you. That's just a twig. This—' Ratan held up the desiccated tail. '*This* was a part of you, once. It still has hair on it. *This.*'

'Ratan, let's go,' said Asif.

Laggulish stretched out a trembling hand for his tail, but Ratan wasn't giving it to him.

'Dr Oak,' Laggulish rasped. 'Come closer, I grow faint, come closer.'

* * *

'Mind he doesn't bite off your ear!'

* * *

Ratan leaned over the bed.

'Dr Oak. *Quercus indicus.* You're just a common creature. How can you understand the joy of being—U—U—'

'Ubermensch?' prompted Ratan.

But the Ubermensch had fallen back, dead.

The Bastard Wing

Ratan couldn't recollect where he had seen her before. Between the dazzle of the sheet and the dull glow of marble, her face floated, unrecognizable. Bruised and bletting, a discard awaiting putrefaction. Beneath the sheet, she was still twenty-five. Perfectly sculpted, perfectly anonymous, perfectly rigid, a medieval apsara uprooted from her native rock. Only the face claimed identity, and yet, it had never looked like this.

Padmini.

He knew her name from Radhakrishnan's call an hour ago. Raki was on his way here. Ratan wanted to be finished by then.

'You want her, Ratan?' Crispin's voice sang out. 'She's yours!'

Crispin was always glad to see him. It took the load off his shoulders whenever Ratan moonlighted at Autopsy.

'I know her face, Crispin—'

'Who doesn't, man? It's been flashed on every news channel all this week.'

A. N. Padmini.

Of course the papers would say Padmini A. N. or Padmini Nosurname. Father's name: Narayan A.

* * *

'Ayilur Narayana Padmini. She looks like her great great-grandfather. Ayilur Narayana Shastrigal. Note the honourific plural—I asked him how many Shastris rolled in one are you?'

* * *

Abruptly, Ramratan was gone, leaving Ratan stranded. All he now had was an extended identity for the corpse.

His phone rang. It was Raki. 'I'm here. Should I wait in your office?'

'No. I'm coming out now.' Might as well put off the autopsy till he heard what Raki, who sounded distraught, had to say.

Padmini stared back at him with discoloured, untenanted eyes.

'You'll be back?' asked Crispin without looking up from the fat man he was busily disembowelling.

* * *

'Clumsy idiot. He's torn the mesentery to tatters already.'

* * *

'Yes,' said Ratan. 'I'll be back.'

He almost walked past Raki who was slumped against a pillar. He followed Ratan in a daze till they sat down in the canteen.

'You've seen the body?' He was barely audible.

'Yes, but I haven't begun the autopsy.'

'It is unavoidable, I suppose?'

'Yes. You know the family?'

'I know the child. Brilliant girl. But then, you know the story.'

'Actually, I don't. All I know is her great great-grandfather's name. Ayilur Narayana Shastrigal.'

That was a jaw-dropper.

Raki was one of the few people who knew Ramratan Oak existed within Ratan's skin. Raki's discovery had been almost simultaneous with Ratan's own realization on 6 December 1992. Since then, Raki time travelled vicariously, every chance he could. A historian by profession, he was Ratan's go to for facts from Ramratan's time.

'Ayilur Narayana Shastrigal,' Ratan repeated.

'*He* gave you the name?'

'Yes. But nothing more. Tell me about the girl, Raki.'

Raki found it difficult to speak. When he finally did, the words were too scant to carry the burden of Padmini's brief life.

'She believed in truth,' he said.

Which might serve as epitaph, but Ratan needed more.

'Why was she in the news, Raki?'

'Because she believed in truth. She made a ruckus at the International Science Congress. The University hosted it this year, you must have heard.'

'Oh yes, I remember reading about it. The Government bestowed its blessing for a session on Ancient Indian Science, right? What was it? Factual mythology? The geography of the Ramayana? Vyasa meets Velikovsky sort of thing?'

'More precisely, Bharadwaja meets George Lucas. That was what she protested. She was working towards a PhD in aeronautics—'

* * *

'Aha! Here it comes, now.'

* * *

'There was a session on ancient aircraft, about how NASA had stolen the wealth of the Saptarishis, and she was to present a paper refuting such claims. At the last minute, she was prevented from reading it. The star of the show was the chap who claimed to have built a spaceship from Bharadwaja's blueprint. Padmini's work would have demolished it. Her paper was about why it just couldn't work.'

'Wait, Raki, slow down. You're telling me this mythical rishi actually left the blueprint for a rocket?'

'Ion thrust engine. That's the label, whatever it means.'

'Come, man, you're the historian!'

'Which is why Padmini wrote to me. To quote her first email a year ago: "After reading your work I've decided you just might be a historian and not a mythologist." We are a dying breed, Ratan. When—if—my book ever comes out, they'll probably kill me.'

'They being the government?'

'I only wish. Vox populi, so assuredly Dei.'

'So what happened when Padmini's paper was refused?'

'She stormed the stage during question hour—and they had to give her five minutes. But when she got to the crux of the matter, they threw her out. So she put up a poster of her equations and schematics. They had that taken down. She picketed right outside the lecture hall, under a "fast unto death for the truth" banner. It went viral over social media—'

'Good, at least she had that.'

'What are you talking about, Ratan? Have you never glanced into that black hole of hate?'

'Never. Why, what did they say?'

'The sanest advised her to watch TV serials to learn the truth about our glorious past. Of course, everybody was certain Western science was one big conspiracy designed to rob us of our copyright on everything from the zero to DNA to genomics. Dark trolls wished her all sorts of hell.'

'Vox populi, eh? She read these comments?'

'Must have. They must have hurt, but not as much as what happened after she was arrested.'

'Arrested? Whatever for?'

'"Preventive" arrest. The university contrived it. She called me from the police station. Her parents had refused to bail her out. Could I speak with them? I was shocked, Ratan. I didn't know her parents were here with her. She's from Bangalore. I knew she was very close to her family, especially to her father. I went to see him immediately. They were parked with relatives in Goregaon. The moment I entered the house, I knew how it would play out.

'The host was at work, his wife and family kept out of sight. Padmini's father, Narayanan, wouldn't meet my eye. Padmini's mother simply wailed. It was intolerable what they had been put through. The shame of it was more than they could bear. They were leaving by the early train the next morning—no reservations, but who cared? It was doubtful if he would survive this.'

'Who would or wouldn't?'

'Padmini's father. His wife was certain his hours were numbered. "All this can be sorted out once Padmini is back home," I said a little roughly. At this, Narayanan said to his wife, "Thank this kind gentleman for me, he has done enough. Now he may leave."'

'"You should come with me to the police station." I stood my ground.'

'"Tell him he is free to go where he wants, but he cannot order me around."

'"Padmini is your daughter."

'"I have no daughter, not any more."

'And so I was dismissed.

'The police were eager to let her go too. She hadn't been charged. She was joking around, eating vada pau when I got there. When she saw my face, the laugh went out of her. I suggested she come home with me, but she wouldn't hear of it. "I'll see this through." She spoke with simple dignity—' Raki seized up.

'Then, this morning, I got a call from her father. She had hanged herself in the bathroom. "Please help us do whatever needs to be done, so that this can be quickly over." Those were the father's words, Ratan. He's coming here in an hour. Can you finish by then?'

'Finish, yes, but I cannot release the body. That is up to the police surgeon.'

'I understand. I just want to know you're certain it was suicide.'

'You're not?'

'I wish I weren't, Ratan. But I know it was suicide. I know the dynamic.'

'The parents tore her to pieces, I imagine?'

'Not at all. We Southerners, we have a different approach towards subversive daughters. Far more effective than name calling or battery or setting them on fire. We don't beat, starve, rape, seclude or kill. We paralyze the will. My mother used to call it psychological murder. I can tell you what happened last evening. Padmini was ignored. Words, protests, tears, threats, all met with an implacable stony silence. Conversations continued brightly, except they all excluded her. At dinner, nobody noticed her. Had she lived, no doubt she would have accompanied them home to Bangalore—where the shunning would have intensified and spread through ranks of relatives and friends. The young would shudder at her contagion. Meanwhile, the parents would receive condolence visits twice a day from people they had never heard of. No guarantee the isolation would not extend to the workplace. Padmini chose the easier way.'

* * *

Ramratan whistled, a low whistle of surprise.

* * *

A shadow fell across their table.

Ratan had been so intent on Raki's narrative, that without Ramratan's whistle, he might not even have looked up.

'Excuse me, you are Ms Padmini's family?'

The man's voice lacked the deference usually granted the bereaved. He was a short globular man in his early forties. His bat ears were bright red from either heat or irritation.

'Myself, Chitale.'

He slid a card on the table.

'Professor D. K. Chitale, Ph.D.' Ratan read out. 'Doctorate in Vaimanik Shastra.'

Chitale pulled up a chair and sat himself down.

'It is a difficult situation,' he observed.

'We are friends of the deceased,' said Ratan. 'Why are you here?'

'Same reason.'

'I see.'

'You are waiting for her father? I also.'

Raki got up. 'I'll be back in half an hour, Ratan. Will that do?'

'Yes.'

* * *

'Let's get back before the father arrives.'

* * *

Despite that, Ratan's feet dragged. What was the point of the autopsy?
Because.

* * *

Because after doing more than a thousand autopsies, I still expect to be surprised.

* * *

As usual, the moment Ratan drew on gloves, Ramratan took over.

Ratan heard him muse, 'I wonder what happened to that Chitale woman...' but asked no questions.

* * *

'Damned if it isn't the same thing!'

* * *

The dead girl's stomach, laid open, had a few small black lumps adhering to its lining. They looked like pills, partially dissolved.

Had she made a half-hearted attempt at poisoning herself, before she chose the rope?

* * *

'No, that wasn't her intent. Of course these may be different, but I'll bet on their contents. *Bacopa monneiri.*

Withania somnifera, nutmeg, cannabis, strychnine.
You name it, it's all here. Same pill, different woman.
Different man?'

* * *

Confusing though this was, Ratan couldn't afford to cloud
the present with conjecture.

By this time he should have grown the familiar headache
which would transport him to Ramratan's time, but that did
not transpire.

The cause of death was the classic hangman's fracture, with
compression of the medulla oblongata.

He dispatched the stomach contents for analysis.

Until that report came in, the death could not be certified
as suicide.

* * *

Raki sat brooding on a bench, far away from the canteen
where Chitale could be glimpsed sharing his table with an
older man—the grief-stricken father, probably.

Before Ratan could speak, Raki handed him a folded piece
of paper. 'She left this for me.'

* * *

*I know you would want me to stay and fight, but I seem
to lack that bastard wing.*
                    ~ Padmini

'I've no idea what she meant, Ratan.'

* * *

'The bastard wing? Ernest's bastard wing?'

* * *

Ratan felt the familiar tug within his skull. The sun made a hot stripe on his forearm, exactly there, at the rising edge of the bastard wing.

* * *

1895

'If you imagine the wing as an arm,' Ernest explained, 'You would look for the bastard wing at the elbow, just beyond the bend of the wing. But, it is actually the thumb. In birds the equivalent of the hand is just three bones welded together, the thumb and the first two fingers. And the stumpy pollux bears the bastard wing.'

'That is vague, Ernest,' Yashoda protested. 'How does a bone suddenly push out a feather?'

Ramratan felt a throb of pure pleasure.

Ernest chuckled. 'A contradiction in terms,' he said.

A rekla stopped at the gate.

Yashoda rose with an exclamation and hurried to the door.

'It's Chitale's wife,' Ramratan said in an undertone. 'You've heard about the fiasco, Ernest?'

He would have given the world to keep the matter from his friend, but he couldn't avoid mentioning it now.

Flight was the most cherished of Ernest's many extravagant dreams. In his dreams Icarus, by day Ernest Hankin pursued a carrion bird. *Gyps indicus*, the Indian vulture, was his closest companion these days.

How would he react to the news that the mystery of flight had finally been solved?

No, a human being hadn't flown yet, but a bird-like contraption had risen to the clouds before a select crowd. That too right here, in Chowpatty. Ramratan unwillingly gave Hankin this news.

The genius who pulled off this miracle was Ganpatrao Digambar Chitale. If he made it to the papers, he would be described as 'a native gentleman of the Brahmin caste'.

'Tell me everything, every detail.' Ernest grabbed Ramratan by the shoulders. 'Tell me everything you saw.'

'I wasn't there, Ernest.'

'You didn't know about it? What, was it a secret?'

Ramratan shrugged. It would have been disloyalty of the worst kind to cheer a man who actually flew while poor Ernest was still running after vultures. He was saved the embarrassment of a reply by Yashoda's return. She looked upset.

'I was just telling Ernest about Chitale's feat,' said Ramratan.

'Chitale's feat?' Yashoda exploded. 'It was his wife Rukmini's feat. And now he blames her for everything! It's now her fault the flying machine fell to the ground and was smashed.'

'Mrs Chitale designed the flying machine?' Hankin asked recklessly.

Ramratan stepped into the breach.

'How high did it fly? Did she tell you?'

'Why don't you ask her yourself? Ernest, she knows you're interested in flight—'

'I'm interested in her!'

'I've just given her a cup of tea, and she's swallowed her headache pills, so give her fifteen minutes to recover, and I'll bring her over.'

'Unbelievable, Ramratan,' enthused Hankin. 'An Indian lady engineer!'

'Why ever not?' Ramratan was as brusque as Yashoda would have been. 'Before she dazzles you, finish what you were telling me about the bastard wing.'

'Eh? Oh that.' Hankin blinked uncomprehendingly at his open notebook. The page was crammed with drawings of wings.

'Is that an archeopteryx? Does it have a bastard wing? Can't you find a less insulting name for it?'

'Alula. It is a prettier name, I agree. No, the archeopteryx lacks one. A poor flier, that one. All modern birds have an alula—whether they soar like the vulture or only manage short flights. So, it definitely does something. But what does it do?'

Yashoda came in with Rukmini Chitale.

Hankin was at his most gallant. He knocked over his teacup, dropped his pen, stammered and turned bright red.

Rukmini appeared entirely unconscious of the effect she had on Hankin.

She addressed Ramratan. 'You weren't at Chowpatty, Yashoda tells me. I thought we sent you an invitation.'

'Yes, I'm sorry I couldn't make it. Mr Hankin here is very interested in flight. He is studying the flight of vultures.'

Rukmini's green eyes focussed on Hankin. 'Then I'm sorry you weren't there Mr Hankin. Perhaps you could have told us what went wrong.'

'What did happen, exactly?'

'The machine flew as designed, kept to trajectory, but it stalled and fell.' Her words were clipped, brusque. 'I failed,' she concluded angrily. 'I need something— something more.'

'Your machine was unmanned, I take it?' asked Hankin.

Rukmini laughed. 'We're ordinary folk, Mr Hankin. Unlike Sir George Cayley, we don't have tenants or dependents who'll risk their necks for us.'

'You're aware of Cayley's work?' Hankin was surprised.

'Why shouldn't we be? He published his ideas almost thirty years ago. But not his designs. My husband wrote to the Aeronautical Society, asking for details.'

'And?'

'Honestly, we did not expect them to reply, so we were not very disappointed.' Rukmini glanced at Hankin's notebook.

He handed it to her.

'These are only birds. I was telling Ramratan about the bastard wing.' He pointed out the small fan of feathers on his drawing of a vulture's wing. 'You can see the alula open as the vulture makes its descent—'

'Alula. I like the name! What does it do, exactly?'

'I don't know. Perhaps you'll tell me.'

'I? I know nothing about birds.'

'But you do about flying machines.'

'Not enough, apparently, or it wouldn't have failed.'

There was such bitterness in her tone that nobody attempted to console her. After a few minutes, she looked imploringly at Yashoda, and, making her excuses, left the room.

Hankin and Ramratan, moved by her turbulence, fell silent.

A rekla was sent for. Rukmini walked towards it as if in a trance. Ramratan put Yashoda's anxiety to rest by taking his seat next to the driver. When he looked back at the dim interior of the carriage a few minutes later, Rukmini was fast asleep.

Ramratan knew the Chitales lived in a small rented flat, but nothing had prepared him for the squalor.

The door was opened by Chitale, and he followed Ramratan to the rekla not to escort but to drag his wife home. He would have shut the door on Ramratan if he hadn't planted his foot over the threshold.

'Vahini appears to be ill,' Ramratan stated.

'Nothing wrong, nothing wrong. Just her nature. Excitable. But I'm controlling it. I have a very good remedy.'

'Really? I would like to see it.'

Unwillingly, Chitale produced a bottle from a mahogany cupboard.

Ramratan poured a stream of brown pellets into his palm. 'These look like goat turds, Chitale. Who gave them to you?'

'I bought them at the Goragandhi down the road.'

Ramratan knew the dispensary. It was run by a dubious vaidya who subsisted on supply and demand.

'You should stop giving her these pills. They will make her dull and tired. She won't be able to work on your flying machine.'

'What does she have to do with my flying machine?'

'Didn't you design it together?'

'Oh, is that what she's been telling you?'

'Not at all. She explained the marvel to us. It is a great achievement.'

Chitale made a rude noise. 'It would have been if she knew what she was doing. All that money wasted. Who will invest now? The Gaekwad was there in person. Four hundred rupees of his money went up in fire before his eyes. He's not such a fool as to repeat the error. But married to a burden like her, what can I do?'

'What did she have to do with the machine crashing?'

'Nothing, nothing. She has nothing to do with my work, understand? She has no respect for where my knowledge comes from.'

'Where does it come from?'

'From the mouth of Bharadwaja Muni. Straight to Chitale, via Narayana Shastrigal.'

'Who's he?'

'Mystic from Madras, presently lodged in Jacob's Circle.'

'And he is in communication with Bharadwaja Muni?'

'Direct communication. To him alone Bharadwaja Muni has spoken.'

'I would like to meet this gentleman. Can you take me there?'

'Impossible. He only speaks Madrasi.'

'There's no such language.'

'Whatever it's called, I can't understand it.'

'How did you understand Bharadwaja Muni?'

'The Muni speaks in pure Sanskrit.'

'I see. If you'll give me the address, I'll try my luck with my impure Sanskrit.'

'I will send you the address later. I've misplaced it.'

'No problem. Good luck with your flying machine.'

* * *

'The rascal is drugging his wife,' Ramratan fumed. 'It's all her work, and he's passing it off as his own.'

'With her consent,' Yashoda observed drily.

'Why would she agree?' asked Hankin.

Yashoda's eyes lit up dangerously. Her face tightened.

'Nobody before my husband, particularly not I,' Ramratan intoned. 'The oldest trick of patriarchy. Women must keep their place.'

'Or be put in it!' Yashoda completed the thought.

'I'm sure it is different in England,' Ramratan consoled Hankin.

'Ask any Englishwoman why she can't vote,' said Yashoda. 'That's the way the world turns.'

An hour later, to their surprise, an urchin delivered a note at Seeta Sadan. It bore no address, was written in English, lacked salutation, and was evidently dashed off in a great hurry.

I think I have the answer to Mr Hankin's question. The alula [do I have the name right?] keeps the wing from stalling at a high angle of attack. As you have observed vultures, you will know how this works in flight.

Thank you for introducing me to the bastard wing.

And here is the address:

Shri Narayana Shastrigal c/o V. Krishnamurthy 25C, D. B. Chawl, Jacob's Circle

'What is this angle of attack?' Ramratan asked.

'It is the angle the chord of the wing makes with the airflow,' replied Hankin. 'She's got something there, Ramratan. Who is this Shastri?'

'The chap who had the revelation which led to Chitale's flying machine.'

* * *

V. Krishnamurthy, whoever he was, was missing. The door to 25C stood open, and its only occupant was a man of about fifty, seated on a mat, reading the *Times*. He looked up at their knock. Certainly, this man was an ascetic, with a lean, almost cachectic frame and a matted topknot of greying hair.

'Narayana Shastrigal?'

The man folded his newspaper with deliberation, rose with some difficulty, and welcomed them.

Leaving them to make themselves comfortable on the mat, he went into the adjoining pantry to return with a jug of water and a hand of bananas.

Having served his guests, he fanned them with a palm-leaf fan as they refreshed themselves.

'There's very little a palm-leaf can accomplish in this airless place,' he said. 'With the sea at your doorstep, why is the air so close?'

'Too many people,' said Ramratan.

'And I one more. Is it me you want or Krishnamurthy? He is not expected home before nightfall.'

'We're friends of the Chitales.'

'Not exactly,' riposted Narayana Shastrigal. 'That man wouldn't have parted with my address unless you got it out of him by a trick. So you do know the Chitales, but they're not your friends.'

'True. Chitale refused to give me your address, but Rukminibai was more helpful.'

'Then I suppose you know she is the aviatrix? She designed that flying machine.'

'Her husband told us it was designed by Bharadwaja Muni.'

'I see.'

It was not clear what he saw. A flash of anger kindled in those calm eyes for an instant, then he laughed. 'So you've come here for the story?'

'You could say that, yes. He told us you only spoke Tamil, and as I don't have that language, I wouldn't understand you.'

'That was no lie. He didn't think I spoke any other language but Tamil.'

'And pure Sanskrit.'

'Another misconception.'

'What is the suffix for? Shastri is evident, but Shastrigal?'

'I'm not responsible for that. I'm plain Narayanan. Others call me Shastrigal. It is the usual plural honourific.'

Ramratan smiled. 'So, how many Shastris are you?'

'I wonder too, sometimes.' The answer was serious. 'I'm overtaken by voices. In languages I do not know. Others call them revelations. I don't know what they are. I can recall them at will, though. One of these is the Vaimanika Shastra.'

'Told to you by Bharadwaja?'

'I'm as skeptical as you are, Dr Oak. You are both doctors, right? When you leave here, you will discuss my diagnosis. Let me know what it is later, if you won't charge me for it. I'm a poor man. Did Bharadwaja speak to me? I don't know. Some tell me it's Bharadwaja. Others tell me it was some other rishi. I wish them luck with their wisdom. I don't know, and I don't care. I tell them if you want this Vaimanika Shastra from me, it is yours. I have no use for it.'

'So you gave it to Chitale.'

'He took notes. Later Rukminibai told me it was of no value.'

'No value to her?'

'Of no practical value, that's what she said. And I believe her. She's an intelligent girl, but she must fight for her intelligence. All of us have to, don't you think?'

'Did you have to?'

'Always. Penury and responsibility are the double yoke every Indian bears. It makes oxen of us in our passivity. To free oneself of all this and think, that's the purpose of life. That's your purpose, isn't it, Dr Hankin? How many ideas have you worked out in your thirty years—or is it twenty-nine?'

'Twenty-nine. Yes, I do like the thought of thinking.'

'So does Dr Oak. But you have freed yourself, and he has not. You can soar like the vultures you study.'

'Who told you I study vultures?'

'Who told me Dr Oak has a special understanding of a certain painter?'

Ramratan was startled now. Alice Kipling had given him Ned Jones' sketchbook when he was thirteen, and since then, those rich introspective colours had become his palette of vision. Nobody except Yashoda knew about this.

'Don't ask me how I know these things. They bombard me from all sides, often in languages I don't know. You spoke of pure Sanskrit. I've never studied the language. The Vaimanika Shastra came to me in Sanskrit. I not only recite it, I understand every word and nuance of it. It is beyond my control. I don't seek to understand it. But I would like it put to use. That's why I travelled to Bombay when someone told me there was a man here who was making a Flying Machine. The truth is, when I arrived here, the Flying Machine was already made—by a woman. But a woman enslaved.'

'He's giving her some pills to keep her quiet,' Ramratan blurted out.

'And she swallows them of her own volition. We make our own lives, Ramratan Oak.'

Ramratan hadn't told him his name, either.

Hankin asked hesitantly, 'Perhaps you have something to tell me?'

Narayana Shastrigal picked up a pen and sketched a design on the margin of the newspaper. Tearing it off, he handed it to Hankin.

'This is a kolam, the apotropaic we draw on the threshold.' Taking the paper back, he drew another. 'This is the screen in a mosque. Both drawings are for you.'

Then rising, again with visible pain, he showed them the door.

'I'll be damned!' Hankin exclaimed as they walked towards Mahalakshmi.

In silent consensus, they sought the sea, clambered over the rocks behind the temple to their usual seat where they could dangle their legs and feel the sea-spray.

'The patterns he showed me have haunted me ever since I went to Agra,' said Hankin.

'Wonder what he'll make of the bastard wing.'

'Keeps the bird from stalling, she said. Maintains lift, but I don't understand how.'

* * *

2015

'Maintains lift, but I don't understand how,' said Ratan.

Raki shook his head.

'The bastard wing. That's what it does. It is a tuft of feathers in the middle of a bird's wing.'

'And you know this because—' Radhakrishnan's voice trailed away in the awe he generally reserved for Ramratan's pronouncements. These rare glimpses of an earlier time nourished him.

Ratan indulged him. 'I just met Narayana Shastrigal. And this Chitale might have something to do with the Chowpatty flying machine. I'll tell you about that in a minute, but there's something more serious here, Raki. I found some partially digested pills in Padmini's stomach. We should have a preliminary report by tomorrow. I cannot release the body till then. Do you have any idea what those are?'

'No.'

'I do. Let's go talk to them.'

Padmini's father looked shell-shocked. Raki introduced Ratan.

'Why so much delay in getting the body?' demanded Chitale. 'Simple suicide.'

Narayanan winced.

'We need some clarity before we can certify,' said Ratan. 'Dr Crispin Quadros is in charge. Please meet him at this time tomorrow.'

'Tomorrow?' Narayanan bellowed in outrage.

'We have to wait for a report on the stomach contents. Your daughter did not eat with you last night?'

'No. I have no idea if she ate anything. Neither my wife nor I did. It was a very upsetting day. I don't want to talk about it now. What's the use?'

'Yes, indeed. You should have talked about it yesterday,' said Ratan. 'With your daughter.'

'Would that have changed her destiny?'

'Simple suicide,' Chitale repeated.

'If it was suicide, then it was an act of will, not destiny,' said Ratan.

'Destined to commit suicide?' Chitale offered.

'Why do you say "if it was suicide"?' Narayanan's words were deliberate.

'Your daughter swallowed at least six tablets—dark brown or black pills. Do you know what medications she was taking?'

'If she was taking anything her mother would have known. I would have too.' Narayanan paused, and then continued with difficulty. 'Before the crazy things she did yesterday, there was nothing Padmini didn't tell us. She is our only child. There's not a thing, not a moment in her life, that didn't fill me with joy and pride. And then—she lost all shame, all decency. Yesterday—'

'Shame? Decency? What are you talking about?' Radhakrishnan demanded.

'You don't know what happened yesterday?' Narayanan asked. 'She made a public spectacle of herself. My wife and I watched everything on the news till the moment of her arrest. We are respectable people. Such notoriety is beyond our imagination. I thought I was going to have a heart attack.'

* * *

'Why didn't he?'

* * *

Before Radhakrishnan could explode, Ratan asked, 'Were you familiar with the paper she was going to present yesterday?'

Both Chitale and Narayanan answered together. 'Certainly!'

'The paper was about our family treasure—my great-grandfather's Vaimanika Shastra. He was not the true author. The text was revealed to him—'

'By Bharadwaja Muni,' Chitale interjected.

'By X, Y or Z, we don't care. We only revere it in honour of my great-grandfather.'

'Narayana Shastrigal,' said Ratan.

Both Chitale and Narayanan evinced surprise.

'I see you know something about the text,' Naryanan observed.

'Perhaps also my role in it?' Chitale said hopefully.

'Well, I do know that in 1895 a flying machine was built by a man called Chitale. He claimed the design was based on the Vaimanika Shastra given to him by one Narayana Shastrigal.'

'Yes and no,' Narayanan stated. 'My great-grandfather said his text had nothing to do with Chitale's flying machine. Padmini learned this text when she was ten. It motivated her study of aeronautics.'

'What was her opinion of the text?' asked Ratan.

'Till yesterday, I thought all her equations and proofs explained the facts in the text.'

'Did she tell you so?'

'Not in so many words. But nothing had prepared me for the way she dismissed it all yesterday. You must have heard her on the news. She called it 'a load of crap.' What did we do to deserve that?'

'Perhaps that was what her equations and proofs revealed,' Radhakrishnan said. 'Padmini was intent on the truth.'

'That is how I raised her.'

'Then you raised her to question and examine.'

'Is nothing sacred?'

'Not to science. And this poses as science. It was her duty to examine its claims to science.' Radhakrishnan's voice was low, intense, cruel, direct. It made Narayanan lower his eyes.

'She was right, but also wrong,' said Chitale. 'She was right about the text. Wrong in how she dismissed it. I told her so. I said she must look at it in proper perspective. She was under too much pressure. I think she was worried also about your reaction.'

'She did not tell you about her paper because you would have disapproved.' Radhakrishnan twisted the knife in relentlessly. 'Her father's opinion mattered more to her than anything else. Your opinion might have prevented her from presenting the paper.'

'She did not present the paper. She was not allowed to present the paper. What was the sense in these high dramatics, in making such a show?' Narayanan cried. 'Padmini was not a publicity seeker. She hated attention of that sort.'

'No, no, she was not after publicity,' said Chitale. 'She told me, "My paper has been thrown out at the last minute because it questions the very existence of Bharadwaja Muni. What business do rishis and devatas have in science? They're a bunch of myths."'

Narayanan sighed. 'Yes, that's what I've taught her. These are beautiful stories, myths designed to question the riddles of human existence, but they are not facts. It is ridiculous to say things like Ganesha was the first head transplant and the Kauravas were test-tube babies. Padmini said the Science Congress might actually feature rubbish like that. I thought she was joking. We laughed about it. God help me, the child spoke the truth!' He clapped his hand to his forehead and sobbed. 'She was just saying what she believed in, what I believe in! Why didn't I see that? Why couldn't I see that?'

'I told her to take it easy,' Chitale said. 'I gave her those pills. Very good Ayurvedic medicine to de-stress. It is our family secret. Especially for ladies. Very good for de-stressing ladies.'

'You get it from the Goragandhi down the road, I suppose?' asked Ratan.

'How did you know?' Chitale was puzzled. 'The same shop has been supplying the family for generations. The only time it has been known to fail was with my great great grandmother.'

'Rukminibai?'

'Oh you know the story? It made quite a scandal in their time.'

'Really? What happened?'

'They quarrelled over Ganpatrao's Flying Machine. What she had to do with it, I cannot imagine! But Ganpatrao was so besotted with her, he let her control everything. The machine crashed, as you probably know. Ganpatrao was certain his wife had sabotaged it somehow. She was a very jealous woman, and

Ganpatrao was a dashing fellow, widely admired. He tried his best to control her. Not very effectively, it seems.'

'With these pills?' Narayanan asked.

'Selfsame pills. The story goes that Ganpatrao made a new design for his aircraft, one that would definitely have worked. His wife hid it and wouldn't part with it. He tried everything, but she was adamant. So he sent her back to her parents, and she died on the way to Sholapur.'

'That is not the truth!' Narayanan said with abrupt certitude.

'What? Are you accusing me of lying?' Chitale's bat ears flamed up.

* * *

'The man is a rat. Looks like one, behaves like one.'

* * *

'I'm saying you're mistaken,' explained Narayanan. 'Ganpatrao did not design anything. It was all Rukminibai's work. She gave the revised design to my great-grandfather. We kept it along with the Vaimanika Shastra.'

'It belongs to *our* family. You must give it to me!' Chitale said flatly.

'If I can find it, it is yours. It was with Padmini.' Narayanan turned to Ratan. 'You're right. We need a report on those pills. When did she take them?'

'Ask why, not when,' fumed Radhakrishnan.

'I will answer to the when,' Ratan said. 'About two or three hours before she hanged herself.'

'Impossible. Those tablets produce a calming effect. They would have put her to a good sleep,' blustered Chitale.

'That may be their advertised effect. They may have acted

differently on Padmini. Psychotropic drugs do that. She was under their influence when she hanged herself.'

Chitale, trembling, picked up a glass of water, spilling it as he tried to sip.

'Calm yourself Chitale!' Narayanan instructed in a cold, oddly high-pitched voice. 'If anybody is responsible for the death of my child, it is me, not you. Radhakrishnan was quite right. The relevant question is not when she swallowed those pills, but why. I rejected her. My wife rejected her. Her piteous appeals ring in my ears now, but I was deaf to them yesterday. We shut her out. We murdered our child.'

He rose and was about to leave when Radhakrishnan said, 'I'll take you home.'

Refusing the offer, Narayanan walked out.

Chitale mopped up the puddle of water with his kerchief. He wrung the cloth out into the empty glass and then held it against his forehead.

'I hope the poor fellow does not follow his daughter!' he said.

'He won't. He'll take the difficult route, and live,' offered Radhakrishnan. 'But your story is still incomplete, Chitale. What happened?'

Chitale shrugged. That was all he knew about Ganpatrao, his disobedient wife, and the failed Flying Machine.

'Padmini sent me her paper yesterday,' Radhakrishnan's voice jolted Ratan back to the canteen table. 'I have it right here. Professor Chitale, you might like to read it.'

'Read it aloud, please,' requested Ratan.

'Yes, certainly. The title is "Legitimizing the Bastard Wing: Aerodynamic Mechanism for the Lift-enhancing effect of Alula". And, what's this? Authors: N. Padmini and Rukminibai Chitale.'

He resumed reading in disbelief:

'The use of the alula in aerodynamic design was pioneered by Rukminibai Chitale in 1895 [Figure 1]. The function of the bastard wing in birds is to prevent stalling at an increased angle of attack. Rukminibai Chitale's drawings incorporate the same design as slats on the leading edge of the wing of a flying machine that was never built.

'This paper shows, experimentally, how the alula works by creating a vortex that allows lift-enhancement at a high angle of attack.'

Chitale read on, but Ratan was no longer listening.

He was no longer even in the canteen. There was steam all around him. He was standing outside the bathroom at Seeta Sadan, waiting for Yashoda to emerge.

* * *

'What happened?' Ramratan asked as Yashoda alighted from the rekla and strode in, stony-faced.

'I must have a bath first.'

The ritual cleansing after visiting a house of mourning.

In this case, not quite the house of mourning. Rumour was Ganpatrao was already seeking a new bride.

The plague had claimed five lives in Ganpatrao's quarter earlier that week. Rukminibai was the sixth.

'Plague?' Yashoda scornfully flung aside his diagnosis as she dried her hair. 'It was those pills. The last few weeks she was comatose, that's what I hear. And not a soul to take care of her, except this devil. What did you say those pills contained?'

'Everything. Opium. Strychnine. Bhang. Brahmi,

and a dozen other things I've never heard of. She might as well have died in a chandol-khana.'

'Why? Why did she crumple like that?' Yashoda's wail beat in Ratan's skull like the relentless slap of the tide.

* * *

'With all her intelligence, why didn't she stand up to this monster? Why couldn't she stay afloat? What did she lack?'

* * *

Only the bastard wing.

Ich Hab Mich Verloren

A heaviness in his hands, that's how he remembered it.

If asked how he had diagnosed the disease that now bore his name, it would be his honest answer: *I felt a heaviness in my hands.*

Of course, that isn't what he would say. He would answer in the words made familiar by print: ... *by the storage of a peculiar substance in the cerebral cortex. All in all we have to face a peculiar disease.*

* * *

Peculiar.

Yes, that was the feeling in his hands that morning, a peculiar heaviness.

16 April, 1906. That was the date they should carve on his tombstone. Nothing else had meaning—the date of his birth, his marriage, his fatherhood; bereavement, misery, recovery. And now, his death? How could these events possibly distinguish his life from a million others? The sine wave of life was universal.

16 April 1906 was the kalends. Everything that followed was brief, compressed into a feverish month of fame, stretched over that morning's frame across nine years, to reach this moment of imminent death.

He returns to it now.

* * *

Monday. A typical Munich Monday. Brittle, not cold. Porcelain skies. The garden tender with early flowers. Birdsong ringing past whispers of morning domesticity. Clink of glass and silver. The approving gurgle of the water closet. Steam. Fresh linen. Coffee and warm bread. The milky scent of children half awake. A whistling cyclist skimming past the window, leaving the tune an endless loop in his brain.

He gets to the laboratory at seven—too early. His impatience seems ghoulish even to himself. Best conceal it here within this glass nautilus, where even breath reverberates.

The conversations of the empty laboratory soothe him. The deep glow of mahogany mirrors past mistakes. The ironic wink of brass reminds him convivial spirits have passed this way. The microscopes locked away in their cases are condensers for his thoughts.

He walks to the shelf of stains. Innocent looking bottles and jars. Their labels announce science, not sorcery. But they hold the magical inks of illumination. These grey crystals, these dark liquids, this muddy crumble of powders, this will conjure up intimacies in the bright eye of the microscope for him, ardent voyeur, to view.

Today he selects potassium dichromate for the first

step of *la reazione nera*. He will take a sliver of fixed tissue, soak it in a 2% solution, and try not to think of it for the next two days. On the third day he will blot it dry, then immerse it in a bath of silver nitrate. Two days later, the speck of blackish tissue will reveal itself as an enchanted forest of arborizing cells.

He had first seen Camillo Golgi's *reazione nera* when he was a student. It transformed the opaque and the unknowable into a dazzling tapestry of black and gold. Golgi was a magician who did not explain his spell. His stain outlined nerve cells with a collyrium of silver chromate. Limned thus, the brain revealed itself as a forest of branching cells, each of which could be traced in its entirety.

In a blink, the depths of the brain had become transparent.

He hopes to do that today — or at least begin the process.

He sets out the stains. Besides Golgi's *reazione nera*, he will try his friend Franz Nissl's method too. Franz, hiding brilliance and broken heart behind his barbed wit, never let on that he had gone one step past Golgi.

Nissl's stains — aniline, thionine, cresyl violet — display the cell's interior.

Everything depends on how far one wishes to go. If Golgi's stain illumines the street, Nissl's takes one into the house. Golgi's *Opera Omnia* has method in detail, but he disagrees with the gestalt.

Golgi considers the brain a loofah where nerve cells mesh with each other in a complex reticulum. That might be believable, if there weren't an opposite view to consider.

The Spaniard Ramón y Cajal has used Golgi's stain to limn that opposing view. Nobody, not even Golgi himself, has used this method of staining with such bulldog tenacity. Cajal has traced nerve cells to their free ends suggesting the brain might be a collection of cells in contiguity, not continuity.

In Cajal's view, nerve cells do not connect structurally. Each remains isolate. Something bridges the isolation. Something Cajal hasn't been able to show. Not yet.

Today he will test out Cajal's idea too.

The brain is on its way from Frankfurt, from the Städtische Irren-Anstalt. It should arrive by eight. Director Sioli has despatched it on the night train.

Yesterday, when he remarked the brain would be here soon, Kraepelin's eyes had widened, his walrus whiskers had trembled — one might have thought he smiled.

'See,' he said gruffly, 'if you can discover the method in her madness.'

To Kraepelin, the methods, or patterns of madness, made up the first and most superficial layer of diagnostics. The second layer was to find the structure underpinning these patterns, as he was convinced the external signs of madness were but projections of underlying disease. The third layer would be to understand the functions of these structural elements. The deepest layer could only be reached when one understood how these functions were carried out. He expected to arrive, one day, at the molecules of madness.

The method of sanity would be a logical beginning, but medical investigation doesn't work like that. The body is reticent in normalcy. It breaks its silence only when something goes wrong.

Of them all, the brain is the most secretive of organs, and madness is its only key.

The brain he's waiting to unlock belonged to a woman who had no secrets.

The wind had whistled through her skull. She had battled to gather her windblown thoughts as other women gather up their windblown hair. Swirling in violent escape, like leaves in a tornado, thoughts had funneled out of her. Orphaned words had clung on, vague and dusty, they cobwebbed her misplaced sentences, and left her anxious eyes searching the air.

* * *

Of their first meeting, five years ago, on 26 November 1901, these are his notes:

She sits on the bed with a helpless expression.

What is your name?
Auguste.
Last name?
Auguste.
What is your husband's name?
Auguste, I think.
Your husband?
Ah, my husband.

She looks as if she didn't understand the question.

Are you married?
To Auguste.
Mrs D?
Yes, yes, Auguste D.
How long have you been here?

Three weeks.

I show her a pencil.

What is this?
A pen.

When she has to write Mrs Auguste Deter, she writes *Mrs* and we must repeat the other words because she forgets them.
The patient is not able to progress in writing and repeats, *I have lost myself.*

Auguste often wore a look of intense concentration, suggestive of deep thought. At other times her face was a mask of anxiety.

The diagnosis was self-evident. Dementia præcox. But Auguste was not syphilitic, and she was too young — fifty-one — to be senile.

For the next five years, he tracked her misfortunes as she lost herself piecemeal, tumbling out of rage into the downslide of helplessness, resignation, inertia, death.

Since his move to Munich two years ago he had noted her deterioration on occasional visits to Frankfurt, but Gaetano Perusini and Francesco Bonfiglio kept track.

He had received their autopsy notes last week.

Exitus letalis: 8 April 1906
Cause of death: Septicaemia as a result of bed sores. Blood poisoning.

He stares at the pages. Instead of Perusini's clean Latin, her face materializes on them, worn and baffled with grief. Strange, before this moment, he has never felt her sorrow. It wounds him now.

A knock.

It is here.

He signs for the box and in his impatience to open it, slams the door in the courier's face.

Director Sioli has packed the jar well in several layers of cardboard and cottonwool. The brain of Auguste Deter floats in formol. He hefts it carefully. It feels soapy. When he sets it down, his hands retain its peculiar heaviness. He pays no attention to that.

He is preoccupied with a new dilemma in his own brain. The battle lines are drawn between good sense and passion. Good sense demands he follow the plan he made an hour ago. A four-day wait for a peep.

Anything can happen in four days.

Three days before Auguste died, Vesuvius erupted, and Naples choked.

He'll go with passion. Bielchowsky's stain, fussy, but quick. He will go with that.

* * *

In the next few hours, he saw things he had never seen before.

He wrote, later:

In the center of an otherwise almost normal cell, there stands out one or several fibrils due to their characteristic thickness and peculiar impregnability.

These fibrils seemed to choke the cell to squeeze out everything else, leaving a tangle of black hair trapping the fragmenting nucleus. In some areas he examined, only these whorls and loops of overwrought fibrils had stayed on as gravestones. The nerve cells were not even noticeable. And, between cells there were blobs he couldn't explain.

A peculiar substance in the cerebral cortex was the best he could do by way of description.

But it was so much more than that.

It was the death of thought.

* * *

19 December, 1915

And it felt like this, a peculiar heaviness in his hands.

We die by degrees, he thought.

He *thought.*

His kidneys had failed, his heart now beat under the patronage of digitalis, he breathed in futile wafts of oxygen, the numbing cold told him his circulation was failing, but, he could still *think.*

His urgency grew frantic.

Before thought ceased, he must understand.

For her, the tangled fibrils, the clumpy plaques, had meant madness. The loss of self. And worse, much worse, the awareness of that loss. In that last awareness there surely lay a trace of thought, before thinking blinked out all together, leaving her vacant as — *what*?

Perhaps she only seemed vacant because he could not read what occupied her.

But hadn't he just *seen* what occupied her brain?

Hadn't he shown up the *structure* of her madness?

Madness was tangible at last, no longer phantom, nightmare, illusion.

He had provided substance to shadow, but what was the nature of it?

Later, Kraepelin said, later, later.

Nine years now to that morning, and the molecule of madness was still undefined.

And he, he was left holding it, a peculiar heaviness in his hands.

* * *

Emil Kraepelin had been quick [some said too quick] to seize on his modest paper 'Über eine eigenartige Erkrankung der Hirnrinde',[1] which he published a year after the great minds of Tübingen had politely dismissed it. It would have gone unnoticed, but for Kraepelin.

Kraepelin had included it in his Lehrbüch, which, already in its eighth edition, was read all over Germany, perhaps all over the world.

He tried to remember what it said:

Although the anatomical findings suggest that we are dealing with a particularly serious form of senile dementia, the fact is that this disease occasionally begins already as early as in the late 40s seems to somewhat to contradict this.

Kraepelin had got even her age wrong. She was 51, not in her early forties, when the madness began.

He did not point this out to Kraepelin.

He couldn't, not after Emil had given the disease his name.

It was an honour hard to bear. There were whispers. Others had seen what he had, and published, too. The litany of these names burdened him: Bianchi, Fuller, Bloch and Marinesco, Redlich, Oskar Fisher.

But Kraepelin had chosen him.

Out of friendship?

---

1. Over a Strange Illness of the Brain Cortex.

In recompense for six years' unpaid labour?

Or in triumph over what he called the 'vapours of Vienna', the psychoanalytic theories of Sigmund Freud?

From Kraepelin's own laboratory came vindication that dementia was not a disordered imagination but a molecule of madness that was choking up the brain.

Kraepelin was a good fellow.

All of them were good fellows. Nissl. Sioni.

And Perusini. Ah, Gaetano!

At the thought of the boy, the heaviness in his hands became leaden. It crept up his arms. His legs were insensate marble. He felt these changes with a rush of welcome.

The telegram had come yesterday.

The boy was dead.

Gaetano Perusini had shared his observations. He should have shared his honour too.

No matter.

It was a poor sort of honour to lend one's name to a kind of madness.

Kraepelin, Nissl, Perusini, they were all redundant.

The children were redundant.

The years, redundant.

Only this conflagrant moment, this moment of vanishing thought was crowded with all the days of his existence.

He saw with astounding clarity the pictures he had captured with his camera lucida.

Dying cells choked by growing tangles of neurofibrils, thick gobs of lipid sitting between cells.

Each cell cut off from its neighbours. Isolation.

In the tangled snarl of neurofibrils, the nucleus lost itself.

* * *

[What was it she had kept repeating? Had it not been something similar?

He could hear her voice, but her words were lost.

He strained to make out the sounds, but they were a distant rustle in the wind.]

* * *

Each cell in her brain had become a stranger to its neighbour. Why did that make her mad?

Hadn't Ramón y Cajal demonstrated already that each cell in the brain was discrete from its neighbour, contiguous yes, but not continuous.

If each of the trillion cells kept its cytoplasm clear of its neighbour's, how did they talk?

Across a synapse.

The word was not much used, and he had never understood whether it meant union or separation, but the paradox fascinated him.

Cells conversed across discontinuities to provide a continuity of thought.

And how did the fibrils and plaques of dementia stop this conversation of *thought*?

His last thought was of how thought sped from cell to cell—unless it got entangled in those fibrils and lost itself.

* * *

The wind brought back her words.

Ich hab mich verloren. I have lost myself.

Thought arrested.

Still straining towards understanding, Alois Alzheimer passed into history.

It was Sunday, 19 December, 1915.

* * *

In 1915, very little was known about the synapse. Another forty years went by before it could be seen on electron microscopy, but by that time the synapse was more than a cleft, a gap between cells.

And today?

Today's synapse is more than a hiatus between two cell membranes.

The molecules of thought are many, and they crowd the synapse.

Alzheimer and Loewi would have marvelled at their diversity, chanted the names like a mantra: glutamate, GABA, glycine.

Those are just the chemicals that excite or inhibit, conclusions to arguments between quarreling factions on each side of the synapse.

Other molecules bridge the cleft between membranes, keep the business going.

The synapse itself rests on a matrix that nurtures it as it matures, and renders it plastic enough to keep going thought after thought after thought.

With so much going on, what can it be but stochastic?

Nations of molecules, each marching to a different drum, come together to make a thought.

Unpredictable, fluctuant, yet falling into step.

Squeezed of space, squeezed of time, multitasking, risky, and with no guarantees.

Everything in the synapse is crammed into less than 300 nanometers. [One nanometer is one-billionth of a meter.]

The synaptic cleft is about 20 nm.

Synaptic vesicles about 50 nm.

Each synaptic bouton contains about 250 vesicles.

Every vesicle has 100,000 of neurotransmitter molecules.

Each transmission takes about 0.5 milliseconds.

A blink, 400 milliseconds.

Thought is so much faster.

* * *

Alois Alzheimer saw amyloid beta peptide plaques in the scaffolding of the synapse, and tangles of tau protein within dying cells, and he thought them the markers of madness.

Forty-six million people alive today have these signs that Alzheimer noticed in two patients.

But in all of them, these are merely byproducts of an earlier, insidious, treachery that disorders the synapse — and arrests thought.

Madness appears as aftermath — but it screams out for attention before it gets noticed.

Alois Alzheimer was asking, *What is it like within the synapse when thought stops?*

Centenary

'Ratan you can't do this.' As Radhika spoke, the network of scars on her face knuckled up angrily in purple corrugations.

'I don't want to,' Ratan shrugged.

Radhika's face changed.

It was like watching some crazy cybermorphing. The scars faded as Yashoda's warm intelligence shone in Radhika's eyes. He should be used to it by now, but it still quickened him with delight.

She laughed indulgently. 'The old man must have his reasons.'

'Old?' Ramratan growled. 'I'll show you old, woman!'

But this morning, the challenge did not end in the usual romp.

It was the sixth of December. Twenty-three years to the day Radhika watched her lover Anwar burn to death. It was the day Ratan Oak's submerged life had burst into the open— the life of Ramratan Oak.

Ramratan Oak, surgeon to the dead, was Ratan's great-grandfather—but that explained nothing.

'Don't explain,' Radhika whispered in his embrace. Now that she guessed where Ratan's decision came from, she no longer opposed it and this made him jealous sometimes.

Now Ramratan chuckled in Ratan's skull. 'That Chikhalkar, complete humbug that he was, couldn't humbug us, could he?'

These days Ramratan stayed long enough to start the conversation that would catapult Ratan into his other life.

'What do you mean?' Ratan demanded.

'Why ask me? You were there. Nineteen fifteen.'

'No, *you* were there, not me.'

'Never mind, we'll both be there at the Centenary.'

'I'm not going.'

'Like hell you're not.'

So he, Ratan Oak, had accepted the invitation from the slime-ball Shakha Pramukh. This had enraged Radhika.

Radhika was the real reason for the invite. She had done nothing to conceal her scars. After a few operations to restore full mobility in her limbs, she had refused any further plastic surgery. She used her scars as a weapon.

'My parents did this to me,' she would say quietly.

It amazed Ratan how seldom the exchange varied.

'Your parents? What did you do to deserve it?'

'My lover was Muslim. I am Hindu. My parents hired a man to burn Anwar to death. I burned too. But I lived. It happened on 6 December 1992.'

Someone invariably said, 'You'll never forget the date...'

And Radhika would shoot back, 'Can you?'

The question confused her listener. 'I?'

'What happened that 6 December? Yes, this happened to me. What happened to you?'

'Nothing. Nothing happened to me on that day.'

'No? The day our nation plunged into fire? Surely, you burned too? These are my scars. Tell me, what happened to you?'

Usually that ended the conversation. And it killed him.

'Must you?' he asked each time.

'I must. It's what I do.'

* * *

Over the years, the neighbourhood's perception of Radhika's scars had changed. She had gone from hero to health warning.

'Earlier, people would say, "Forgive your parents." Nowadays they say, "Time heals everything, na? By now your parents must have forgiven you."'

The local Right was celebrating the birth centenary of Pandurang Chikhalkar, and for the heartbeat of Bharatvarsh to resound in the ears of aliens and barbarians, invitations were sent to 'trouble-makers' too.

It was typical of them that the invitation should be addressed to Ratan Oak, with 'and family' crossed out in red ink.

Ramratan wanted him to go, but Ratan was not as easily persuaded as Radhika.

No matter what Ramratan's view of Chikhalkar was, he would have to sit through an hour or more of cringe-making adulation, and then one more of listening to the poet's propagandist effusions recited, or even worse, sung relentlessly off-key.

'I'm not going,' he let Ramratan know. 'Why should I care if a third-rate poet turns hundred?'

Ramratan laughed. 'Hundred? He would be my age if I were alive. It is not a birth centenary, it is *the* centenary.'

'Of what?'

'The celebrated poem Chikhalkar wrote in anguish. He gave it to his son sealed in a porcelain bottle on 6 December 1915.'

'How do you know it was a porcelain bottle?'

'Our Kaviraj couldn't swallow his bhakri without a dab of *Patum Peperium*.'

'What on earth is that?'

'Some kind of fish paste. Nasty, expensive stuff. Nusser saves his jars for Yashoda. Neat round porcelain screw-top jars.'

'Why not seal the poem in an envelope?'

'Ha! Chikhalkar wasn't looking for convenience. His quest was always for immortality.'

'Time capsule.'

'The term is new to me, but yes. Time capsule. Gentleman's Relish as time capsule,' Ramratan laughed. 'Can't miss that, can we?'

'What's in the poem?'

No answer was forthcoming.

Ratan felt the familiar migraine setting in. Since he had given up fighting it, he preferred to time travel in comfort. He kicked off his shoes, and looked around for a cushion. He hadn't noticed till now how annoyingly his neck ached...

* * *

1915

He hadn't noticed till now how annoyingly his neck ached. He seemed to have lived with this excruciating pain all his fifty-five years. Would the ride never end? His fingers itched to take the wheel from Nusser. Perhaps he should strangle him first. If it hadn't been for the humbug in the back-seat, he would have done one or the other. Ramratan clenched his teeth as Nusser hit another pothole.

The Silver Ghost was getting it much worse than his neck.

'…the chassis has been specially developed for Indian roads,' Ramratan quoted silently from the luxurious brochure, but both Rolls & Royce had reckoned without Nusser.

The expedition was all his own fault.

Darayus Surveyor had shown him a marvel when he was thirteen. Nusser, a sickly boy, never made it to these field trips with his geologizing father, but Ramratan accompanied Darayus every summer.

Darayus was a wonderful teacher. He would bring alive the Sahyadris like a storybook without an ending.

Nusser had missed it all.

He couldn't care less, but Ramratan felt the entire weight of the ghats oppress him after Darayus's death, and never lost an opportunity to restore Nusser's patrimony.

So when Nusser had announced a 'country jaunt' to break in the Silver Ghost, still gleaming untouched in his bungalow at Aundhgaon, Ramratan suggested they drive down to the Kukdi riverbed, 'Our own, very private Hawaii, pāhoehoe in Poona!'

And despite Ramratan's pleading, Wilson was given the day off, and they set out at dawn with Nusser driving.

'We're picking Chikhalkar up on the way,' said Nusser after a bumpy mile. 'Flows like silk, doesn't she, Ramratan?'

'Why?'

'It's all about the engine—'

'Why Chikhalkar? Why that insufferable bore?'

'I can't stand him either. He begged, Ramratan, and I can't stand that too.'

'Yes, but what for?'

'He said he'd never been in a motor, as he calls it.'

'Isn't it against his principles? This is a western invention.'

'Not at all. He says Henry Ford got the blueprint for his engine out of the Ramayana.'

'No, those were the Wright Brothers. They stole the pushpak viman.'

'Don't rile him, Ramratan. Promise me you won't.'

'That's rich, Nusser. First I must endure him, and then promise not to rile him? Why?'

'Because if you do, he'll start reciting his stuff.'

That silenced Ramratan.

* * *

They found Chikhalkar waiting for them at the Koregaon-Bhima naka, holding forth to an adoring audience of chelas.

'Hop in! We're in a hurry,' said Ramratan unguardedly.

Nusser groaned.

On cue the chelas struck up Chikhalkar's popular, *Where so fast, O traveller?* The punch line was delivered with fine irony:

Twenty horses to your engine?
What, twenty?
My chariot has just two and two's aplenty!

'Does that mean you'll walk?' Ramratan asked.

Chikhalkar ignored him. He silenced his chelas and trotted them around the Rolls Royce.

'Today we will call this a motor car,' he declaimed. 'We may even concede it to Rolls & Royce. But the time is not distant, my friends, when it will be called by its true name. Vidyut Vahan! So, don't say RR, say VV!'

'VV!'

Nusser took this as a signal to rev up and the chelas fell back in alarm.

Chikhalkar was posted into the back seat complete with umbrella, cloth bag and shining brass kamandal.

For the first ten miles or so, the sheer tumult of the journey silenced Chikhalkar's muse, and he mercifully nodded off.

Ramratan divided his irritation between Nusser's driving, his aching neck, and the long miles ahead.

They halted for lunch at noon.

Wilson had done them proud: rugs, cushions, a tall canister of water and not one, but two, wickerwork hampers that promised all sorts of delights.

'Two hampers, Nusser?' asked Ramratan. 'Isn't that excessive?'

Silently, Nusser pointed to the poet who still snored, huddled in Nusser's shawl.

Shuddha shakahari, no doubt.

Ramratan stretched his legs gratefully. Nusser tore off his goggles, cap, traveling coat and settled down on a rug.

'We should let Chikhalkar sleep,' suggested Ramratan.

But Nusser, kindly host, would have none of it, and Ramratan woke him none too gently.

Chikhalkar trotted off into the bushes, kamandal in hand, and returned with a brisk air of appetite.

He waved away the shuddha shakahari hamper as a childish affectation.

'The road has its own dharma,' he proclaimed as he tucked into the sandwiches.

Wilson had relied on the Royal's very British largesse.

'Roast beef,' Ramratan warned.

Chikhalkar nodded happily and took one more. He was lavish with mustard and pounced on the little pot of Patum Peperium with a cry of joy.

'This is my favourite,' he confided, as he slathered it indiscriminately on everything he ate, and as he ate everything, the pot was soon wiped clean.

Wilson had indulged Ramratan by providing little ramekins of his delectable crème caramel.

'Such tiny servings!' Chikhalkar complained. So they gave him theirs too.

'I'm taking a walk.' Ramratan set off brusquely, but before long Chikhalkar joined him.

'Nusser is taking a nap,' he said. 'This kind of lunch is most stupefying to the brain. Leaves one in tamasik gloom!'

'I suppose your satvik glow comes from all the rajasik things you've eaten?' Ramratan riposted.

'Listen, don't get me wrong, but will your friend mind if I take two of those dabbas of ghee?'

'Foie gras? Ask him, I'm sure he won't mind.'

'It is highly recommended in Ayurveda.'

'No doubt. So too are elephant testicles and tiger pizzle.'

'For advanced cases only. In my case this ghee induces poetic fire.'

'Really? The fat-engorged liver of a goose can do that for you?'

'You're the doctor, not me. And there is nothing satvik about poetry.'

'The other two, eh?

'Sometimes one, sometimes the other. Look at those women now. I may stare at them, and though I am on fire, my gaze is blameless, for I am a poet. You, on the other hand can have nothing but lust in your gaze, you not being a poet.'

'Still, I suggest you stop staring unless you want a thrashing.'

'They're going to thrash me? Those little chits?'

'No. I will.'

Ramratan turned away in disgust. He bumped against something and nearly lost his balance. It was a slab of granite too strange to be a milestone.

The carving on the stone arrested him. A woman's upraised arm, displaying the unbroken bangles of conjugal felicity.

A sati stone.

Judging from the crude unembellished carving, the sati was a humble villager, her life rendered significant only by death.

Sati stones were common enough in the countryside, but he could never stop the dread that overcame him when he saw one. There but for the grace of God went Yashoda—

'How shameful to let it lie where our feet touch it!' Chikhalkar exclaimed. 'Those women just walked past it! They should be worshipping this punyavati, lighting a lamp, anointing it with haldi and kumkum, garlanding it with flowers. Surely they've earned the wrath of this pure soul.'

'Let's go, Chikhalkar.'

'You carry on. I'm not going anywhere till I've shown these women the error of their ways!' And he grimly marched ahead, every slap of his chappals a scold.

Ramratan was strongly tempted to return to the car and urge Nusser to take off, leaving this nuisance behind. Only the fear of Chikhalkar saying or doing something offensive made him follow.

Chikhalkar was in mid-harangue when Ramratan caught up with him. The three women looked too frightened to respond with anything more than looks of distress. They were very young, barely in their twenties.

Ramratan managed to get a word in and pressed his advantage by asking them about the village.

But Chikhalkar's rebuke had awoken something deeper than alarm in them.

'Is that why you've come?' the first girl asked hesitantly. 'For the ceremony?'

'What ceremony?' Ramratan's mouth went dry.

'That.' The girl pointed to the fallen sati stone.

'Is there such a ceremony today?' Ramratan forced out the words. 'For whom?'

'In the Patil's house. They say it's his daughter-in-law. But we don't know anything about it.'

She was about to pull her friend away, but the other girl turned suddenly brave. 'No, we know about it. We watched them build the hut.'

'Hut?'

The girls would say no more, but Chikhalkar seemed to know all about it.

'The hut is good,' he said with approval. 'With a hut, everything goes off well. Come on, let's watch the fun!'

'We aren't going to watch. If you want to, we'll show you the way.'

The girls set off, hurrying more to escape Chikhalkar than to get anywhere.

It couldn't be happening—

* * *

Ramratan was already running, heart in mouth, in the direction the girl had pointed. It couldn't be happening, but he knew it could.

Chikhalkar came loping after him, pointing importantly at the knot of people gathered in the distance. 'That must be it.'

Ramratan, who had paused for breath, set off again, with Chikhalkar close on his heels. It crossed his mind that Chikhalkar's motives might be very different from his own. 'Slow down, Oak! I can tell you there's plenty of time.'

'How would you know?'

'I say—you're not going to do something foolish, are you?'

'I'm going to stop it.'

'It is a noble act, sanctioned by the scriptures. You have no right to stop it.'

'It is murder. For your information, it is not sanctioned by any old scripture. And, what if it were? If you die tomorrow, would you want your wife to burn herself with your body?'

'I would. But she probably won't. It is her choice. Look, there's the hut now.'

'What's this hut for?'

'The husband's body is placed inside the hut. The widow is led in, and the thatched roof is weighted down with logs. Then the door is barricaded with more logs. The true punyavati will light the pyre herself, from inside. So I've heard. I've never seen one myself. Bruce Carlisle Robertson made the hut famous, you know.'

'Who's he?'

'Used to be the Sahib here a century ago. He tried to stop sati. Naturally, the people didn't like his interfering. So he tried another trick. He got them to alter the hut in such a manner that the logs wouldn't fall in at once, and the woman could escape, if she wanted to. He witnessed what happened when they tried it his way. The hut exploded within seconds! He became the laughing stock of Poona!' Chikhalkar laughed heartily.

Ramratan had never before felt such revulsion

towards any man, and yet he grabbed Chikhalkar by
the arm and said earnestly, 'We've got to find her.'

The poet tried to shake free, but Ramratan dragged
him along in his stride.

A purohit was readying the grass hut. He stopped
them angrily, barring their way towards the hut.

'You're perfectly aware you're committing murder,'
Ramratan said coldly. 'I'm a government official and I
will have you arrested within the hour.'

Several voices shouted back. 'We don't know you.
You have no authority here.'

'I do.' Nusser stepped forward. 'I'm a magistrate.
When I say stop, you stop. Dr Oak and I will have the
police here before you know it.'

Ramratan was surprised by Nusser's sudden
appearance, but not by his quick grasp of the situation.
It took a crisis to bring out his genius.

'We're not forcing her,' said a young man. 'She's
doing it because she wants to. Because it is the right
and noble thing to do. Isn't that the truth, vahini?'

The woman he addressed, a stout girl in her thirties,
nodded enthusiastically.

'Yes, it's always been her intention. And now, none
of us can stop her.'

'How did her husband die?'

'Snake bite. She will be very upset if you stop her
now.'

'Let me speak with her.'

They were intimidated by Nusser's authority and
Ramratan was led, unwillingly, into a house some
distance away.

Their guide pointed to a darkened room. 'She's in
there.'

The others fell back.

Ramratan pushed open the nearest window when he entered the room. Behind him Chikhalkar gasped in disbelief.

A small girl dressed in wedding finery sat crouched against the wall.

Ramratan froze.

The child was barely fifteen.

She cowered and shrank into her clothes under their scrutiny.

Ramratan knelt down next to her.

'Don't be frightened, little one,' he murmured. 'Do you know why you've been brought here? Tell me.'

Her eyes focused severely on him. A small voice asked 'How long will it hurt? They say it won't hurt at all. The fire won't burn me. I'll go straight to swarg.'

'No, that is a lie. The fire will burn you. It will hurt worse than the worst pain in the world. That's why I won't let it happen to you. Come on! I'll take you home to your parents.'

'No! They'll be angry with me! I'll bring shame on them!'

That canard. Would it never stop?

'Come on, now.' He raised her in his arms and carried her out.

A sobbing woman was being led towards them. She took the child wordlessly from Ramratan.

'The police will be here to make enquiries,' Nusser told the spectators. Nothing could have made them disperse quicker.

'Let's go home,' Nusser suggested.

Ramratan nodded. The Kukdi river bed could wait.

Chikhalkar stumbled after them.

They passed a small temple where the same purohit was in attendance.

Chikhalkar stopped for a moment to peer at the murti in the dark sanctum.

'Why have you draped a sari over the devi?' he demanded.

The purohit answered with a scornful look.

'Why?' persisted Chikhalkar.

'Why? For decency, what else?'

Chikhalkar, quite satisfied with that answer, caught up with them and the Silver Ghost set off at a bone-rattling pace.

All three men were silent.

* * *

Nusser's abstraction made him drive better.

Ramratan, battling his own demons, ignored both his aching neck and Chikhalkar's attempts at conversation.

At Koregaon-Bhima, Chikhalkar insisted they stop by his house for a few minutes as he wanted them to witness something important. Wearily, they agreed.

Chikhalkar invited them to be seated on the stone bench in the verandah and called for his son.

'Bring my desk!' he barked when the boy turned up.

The desk was brought.

The poet scribbled a few lines on a piece of paper.

'Now, my friends. I would like you to witness this. I have just written, under your scrutiny, the most important poem of my life. It contains not my dreams, but my conviction of what my dreams will accomplish. Not today or tomorrow, but a hundred years from now! So, in your presence, I'm sealing this poem.'

And from his pocket out came the emptied Patum Peperium jar from Nusser's picnic.

The poet folded his poem and put it into the jar still cloudy with fish paste. Then, taking a stick of red wax from his desk, he sealed it securely.

'There, Madhav! This is your responsibility. And your son's, after you. In the presence of these honoured gentlemen, I entrust you to open this one hundred years from today. On 6 December, 2015! Then the world will understand the burden oppressing my soul today.'

Without further ado, he politely thanked his visitors, and sent them away.

'The arrogance of the man!' Ramratan gnashed his teeth.

Nusser guffawed. 'He's a poet, Ramratan, forget him.'

But they were to remember him, after all.

* * *

2015

'He blamed me for his suicide,' Ramratan's voice continued in Ratan's brain.

'He committed suicide?'

'Within the month. It was called an accident, naturally. He was cleaning a pistol. That was seen as political. If the gun hadn't gone off in his face, Chikhalkar, not Mohandas Gandhi, might have been the Mahatma responsible for free India.'

'Why blame you? Did he leave a note?'

'No. He blamed me long before that. The letter came on Christmas Day. I've kept it somewhere, you'll find it. A lot of blather about Bharatvarsh, but the lines meant for me said:

On you rests the entire responsibility for my despair. In that one afternoon you cremated all my dreams. Scorched by their embers, my fingers have written the truth at last, but you will not be around, my friend, to read those lines.

'The Patum Peperium bottle?'

'Yes. You see now why we must go for that Centenary?'

Ratan was received at the entrance by a bevy of young women all clad in colourful nauvaris.

He was faintly surprised to identify a couple of his own students among these apsaras. Escape was now impossible.

An arati was waved at him, a tilak bestowed, a rose offered as boutonnière, his hair sprayed with rose water.

Young men in tasselled dupattas and saffron phetas bustled around importantly.

One of them approached Ratan with folded palms. 'We're greatly honoured by your presence, sir. Please take your place on the stage.'

Pinioned between two other boys, Ratan was literally dragged to the podium.

'Why are you so important all of a sudden, Ratan?' Ramratan sounded alarmed.

The guests already seated on the podium rose to greet Ratan.

'That's the grandson.' Ramratan identified the youngest Chikhalkar. 'I'd know that snub nose anywhere.'

In a daze, Ratan subsided into the plastic chair. He registered nothing till his name boomed back at him from the microphone.

'...and we are privileged to have with us, Dr Ratan Oak, the torchbearer of none other than that fearless champion of truth, Purushottam Nagesh Oak! Here is the man who will restore to our Hindu Rashtra the great, the glorious Tejo Mahalaya! Yes, the sacred temple we have been swindled into calling the Taj Mahal! But that must wait. On that day, Ratan Oak, we will greet you with our hearts in our extended hands. But today's ceremony is no less important. I will now ask Shri Mohanrao Chikhalkar to introduce the Time Capsule.'

'Sit down!' Ramratan whispered furiously.

Ratan, who had every intention of bolting, stayed.

'Who is this new lunatic? He's no relation of ours!'

There was no time to answer Ramratan as just then Chikhalkar's grandson, a man in his eighties, rose to great applause. He swayed on his feet and had to be persuaded to deliver his speech sitting down. It took a while to get him started.

'My father has often spoken of the day when my revered grandfather wrote this poem,' Mohan began. 'He had spent the day on a padayatra through our glorious countryside. As you know, every grain of our punyabhumi was a syllable to him, every blade of grass a punctuation mark, every flower a song—'

Enthusiastic clapping greeted this effusion.

'So, it happened like this. That day my grandfather had walked many miles, supported by his friends who hung eagerly on his every word, urging him to write a new poem. Can that be done on order? Never! But my grandfather told my father that this poem, the one that will be revealed to the world today by my unworthy self—this poem was compelled by what he had seen and heard that day. It was an effusion from the very depths of his soul. You know how the simple joys and sorrows of humble people made up the lifeblood of his poetry.' Overcome, Mohan Chikhalkar mopped his forehead.

An ornate casket of gilded cardboard was now placed before him and opened to great cheering.

He took out a small porcelain jar and held it up.

'I want you to see this! The sealing wax is undisturbed. It has been undisturbed for a hundred years! From 6 December 1915 till today. I ask you, have I kept this sacred trust to the people's satisfaction?'

'Yes!' roared the audience.

'Then I have not lived in vain. It has been my life's endeavour to see this day complete.

'Get on with it, you idiot,' hissed Ramratan.

* * *

Shouts of 'Open it!' urged Mohan's fumbling attempts to break the seal.

The master of ceremonies and other worthies crowded him, and under their joint efforts the Patum Peperium jar fell to the floor and shattered.

A folded scrap of paper fluttered away in the fan's waft.

Ratan dived hastily and handed it to Mohan, who was being restored with a glass of water.

Mohan settled his spectacles, and in taking the paper he retained his hold on Ratan's hand to draw him into the chair next to him.

Ratan was concerned about the man.

Mohan was breathing uneasily, his forehead was pouring out rivulets of sweat. But he grasped the mike with greed and cleared his throat as he opened the paper.

Over his shoulder, Ratan read the poem with disbelief.

Ramratan chuckled. 'Here comes my absolution, Ratan.'

Mohan laughed.

It was a short, scornful laugh that transformed him.

He rose energetically to his feet and spoke in a strained yet steady voice. 'The poem is in English. Does that surprise me? No! No man is a prophet in his own country. So he wrote his prophecy not in the sweet tongue of his birth, but in the brutish language of the tyrant. It is a short poem, only four lines. He told my father that it would be the song of the times, shouted from rooftops, lisped by infants in their classrooms. Yes! Listen carefully and judge for yourselves—

'We battled long, and awfully,
To lose the past we loathed—'

Mohan repeated the lines with growing fervour till the audience chanted it with him. His thin voice swelled to a rich baritone as he declaimed the entire quatrain:

'We battled long, and awfully
To lose the past we loathed.
Brides may now burn lawfully,
And all our gods are clothed!'

A stunned silence followed.

Ratan wondered if Mohan Chikhalkar had quite grasped the lines he had read so powerfully.

As if in answer, his voice rang out again, and the audience joined in.

Soon they were all chanting, like a mantra of redemption, Chikhalkar's anthem for a lost dream.

We battled long, and awfully
To lose the past we loathed.
Brides may now burn lawfully,
And all our gods are clothed!

The Castle of Insanity

If not for the sudden cloudburst, Ratan would never have entered the art gallery. Till he pushed past the glass door, he thought it was one of those arty cafés that spring up like fungi in this season and last just as long. Art had few takers in this part of town. Art galleries were for clothes: limp shalwar qameez that a headless mannequin had fled, or luminescent trousseaux winking out a long half-life, awaiting the prince.

But there were no clothes here. It, really, was an art gallery.

Its dim wedge of space relied on the glass wall for lighting. In rainy weather, it was no help at all.

The place was empty. Ratan noticed an iron stepladder. Presumably there was someone hidden in the loft. The ubiquity of cameras allowed that.

In glowering light the paintings had become squares and rectangles of shadow on a dun wall. A wrap-around abstract, its restricted palette the nothingness of space. Or dust. Or space dust, Mondrian khaki.

Ratan was transfixed. The tangled day slid off, his skin absorbed emptiness. A wordless peace filled him.

It was exhilarating. He was a zillion cells on tiptoe, powering for take-off. Any moment now he might turn weightless, and launch into infinitude, exploring pockets and crevices of shadow in the emptiness. He could feel its flavours on his tongue, hear its music. Its charge surged, electric and erotic, arrested just short of apogee to leave him intensely alert on the shining edge of a swoon.

Ratan moved his head to the left, and the tail of his eye caught an errant flash. The next instant, he was no longer there.

He stood now at the edge of a road, facing a wall. Its top glowed like a red-hot wire. How dark it was on this side of the wall, and how bright beyond. He must look over the wall, he decided. In the murk, it was impossible to find a foothold. If only he could find a boulder or a brick to stand on, he could reach the top, and haul himself up. As he thought this, Ratan found he could easily see over the wall.

At the same time, and uneasily, he was aware of himself in the art gallery, rooted before a painting. That awareness was telescopic, like the momentary glimpse of an incidental memory. From his vantage at the wall, the distant moon was more immediate than his mud bespattered self. The moon was a bright little saucer holding up a pale grey egg. It floated between dark shapes that might be trees. Or not. What they actually were seemed unimportant, but their accretion limned the sky against the brightness beyond the wall.

* * *

Although he could now see over the wall, Ratan didn't. It seemed more important, more urgent, to absorb his immediate surroundings. There were no stars, or he could have mapped the sky. He scrutinized the gradations of grey that composed the darkness in a necessary prelude to finally looking over the wall.

The extreme self-indulgence of this delay pushed him closer to that keen edge of pleasure that he hoped would leave him there, quivering, at the precipice.

Eventually, he looked over the wall.

It was everything he knew he would see.

A large tree, its perfect umbel lit by the lamp that illumined all. The foliage cast shadows intricate as lace. The dazzle of the lamp obscured everything behind it. The ground, bare, brown, cracked, swirled purposefully down towards the wall. The patch of brightness seemed to intensify under his gaze, and then, abruptly, extinguished itself.

Ratan felt his heart stop. He panicked that he had turned blind. The darkness was absolute. Fear paralyzed him. It was only when he felt his fear retreat did he discover that light had begun to creep in again.

The lamp no longer shone, but a pale glimmer breathed and outlined the tree. The grey beyond assumed shape. It was a house, a two-storeyed bungalow. The tree was just embroidery now, against its squat solidity. The light seeped out from its windows, first one, then another, as if the inhabitants took turns to switch on lights in room after room after room.

The fear that he was trespassing nagged at him, but he could not leave.

The windows glimmered on and on, faster now, with a rising desperation.

Then they all went out for a beat, a heartbeat, his.

A brightness appeared, wavered, settled into a diffuse glow, and he saw, very distinctly, a room opening to a balcony. There was a woman in the room. He saw her dimly, surprisingly so, for the room was bright enough.

She emerged into the balcony, and he saw her perfectly now.

Her uplifted face strained at the darkness. There was anguish in the tensile stem of her neck, in the fragile shoulders above the hazy tides of her sari. The breeze ruffled her hair as she leaned forward on the railing.

For one terrible moment Ratan thought she was going to jump.

She seemed to peer through the darkness, straight at him.

She held out her hands in piteous appeal, her mouth moved silently.

The light went out.

Ratan knew she was lost to him.

* * *

'Unforgettable,' said Ramratan in Ratan's ear. 'I thought it would be gone by now, but it keeps coming back to me.'

'What is this place?'

'Irrenschloss.'

* * *

He knew the word—or did he?

* * *

He knew the word—or did he?

Ramratan straightened and took Mueller's pulse once again. It still raced in fits and starts.

'He should be quiet in about half an hour,' said Nusser. 'Let's go get that breakfast Cajetan has been nagging about.'

Mueller had poached Cajetan from the Byculla Club. It was no mean thing landing a cook with an European reputation, nevertheless Mueller had to endure a great deal.

The depth of Cajetan's loyalty had come as a surprise.

When they brought Mueller home, Cajetan had cleaned and restored him to a semblance of normalcy with the mechanical efficiency of a hospital matron. After they had got him into bed, Cajetan stood in the shadows like an effigy, waiting for orders. When none came, he muttered something and walked off into the kitchen. He appeared half an hour later to announce that breakfast was served.

'It's five in the morning!' protested Nusser.

'Better eat now. Or where will you find the strength to look after Sahib?'

It was now a little past six and Cajetan had kept up his nagging for an hour.

'Come on, let's eat his Frenchified eggs,' Nusser urged. 'These cooks are temperamental people.'

Ramratan was about to follow Nusser out of the room when Mueller uttered the word again.

'Irrenschloss.'

This time Nusser heard it too.

'What does it mean, Nusser?'

Nusser didn't know either.

At the table, Cajetan's first offering was not Frenchified eggs. He plonked down a tattered volume before Nusser. It was a German-English dictionary.

'You're learning German, Cajetan?'

'Irrenschloss, bitte.'

'Castle of Insanity?'

'Sounds about right. Let's hope Mueller can explain it.'

They worked their way through oeufs en cocotte, brioche and coffee, as Cajetan watched over them like a lynx, grimly persisting in refills at their every attempt to end the meal. Finally, he was convinced that was enough strengthening.

'Now tell us Cajetan.' Nusser spoke in what Ramratan called his Kaiser voice. Generations of feudal patronage fortified that gentle tone. Infallibly, it commanded obedience.

Cajetan's story was quickly told.

Otto Mueller had taken to nocturnal rambles over the past month. He overslept, abandoned his breakfast, and clattered at breakneck speed to Elphinstone College to be in time for the early lecture. When he had actually missed two lectures Cajetan had the following exchange with his master:

'Sahib is tired of Cajetan, I think?'

'Why should you think that, Cajetan?'

'Then why you're making me look for another job?'

'Am I? Not to my knowledge.'

'Whole world knows I am Major Domo of Professor—'

'My only Domo.'

'But of Professor, no? If no longer Professor, then who will pay Domo?'

Having thus warned Mueller that his Professorship was in peril, Cajetan, for Mueller's own good, decided to snoop on him.

This turned out to be more difficult than anticipated.

Mueller only left the house an hour after midnight, and he drove his own carriage. Cajetan lacked the means to follow him on the first few nights, but two nights ago he had managed to borrow a bicycle.

The first night on the cycle was disastrous. He fell ingloriously at the first bump and cut his forehead. Next morning it was difficult to endure Mueller's advice on temperance, but that only made Cajetan more intent.

He practiced all afternoon on the bicycle, and by midnight he was out and waiting in the shadows for Mueller to emerge.

It was a rough ride. There were few streetlights for the first mile and then none at all. The moon was a chancy blur, the road unmetaled.

Somehow Cajetan kept up. He had lost his bearings, though. When the carriage stopped at last, he was clueless about the location.

Cajetan had expected a chakala, a brothel of some sort, but this was far removed from the sleeping streets he had flown past an hour ago. His calves hummed as if bumblebees were trapped within the skin. He felt as though he had pedalled halfway across the earth.

Mueller walked some distance from the carriage and looked up. Something like a wall loomed ahead of them. His white face, uplifted, was clearly visible. Cajetan thought it politic to stay where he was and wait for Mueller's expedition to unfold.

Mueller grew impatient, paced about, swishing the whip. There was an energy to that swish which alarmed Cajetan. His master was here for revenge, not love. Cajetan began to wish he had brought along his nephew, a burly fellow, and biddable [the bicycle was his]. On his own, Mueller couldn't have frightened a rat.

His thoughts made Cajetan as impatient as Mueller. Every five minutes or so he caught a gleam as Mueller examined his watch.

Then Mueller startled and gave a small cry. It was the sound of hopeless expectation.

Cajetan relaxed. It wasn't revenge after all. Only love produced a cry of that sort.

A light floated up some distance away. From its height, Cajetan deduced it must be the second storey. Which meant there was a bungalow. With a lady inside.

The lady carried a lamp from window to window, and Mueller followed it. There were many windows and the lady moved quickly back and forth, making Mueller dance like a pendulum.

The light went out.

Mueller lingered for a while. Then he walked morosely back to the carriage.

The journey home was so slow Cajetan was afraid Mueller would spot him.

* * *

The next night, Mueller went out again.

Again Cajetan followed.

This time Cajetan quite enjoyed the ride.

Mueller had carried a lantern, and this time, Cajetan saw the lady.

She came out on a balcony.

To Cajetan's surprise, she was not a mem, but 'normal Indian lady' in a sari. Her hair flowed in loose waves like a river in twilight, her eyes burned like stars, her lips were rose petals.

Did Cajetan see her face so distinctly?

Not really.

Her face was just a blur. He deduced all this from Mueller's attitude.

Mueller had fallen on his knees. Head thrown back, arms outstretched, he embraced her across the darkness.

Cajetan heard him sob.

The lady on the balcony saw him.

Dropping the lamp, she too flung out her arms yearningly.

The lamp went out, and Mueller was left straining at the dark.

* * *

Cajetan did his best to console Mueller. He gave him käsekrainer for breakfast.

'Very famous German sausage. Very delicate, not like our Goan rubbish!' Cajetan explained to the ignorant.

Nusser nodded humbly and requested him to continue.

Mueller ate the käsekrainer. Out of terror, Ramratan suspected.

Mueller had often remarked that unappreciated meals brought about cruel repercussions. He had once lived on burnt toast for a week after passing up a second helping of boeuf bourguignon.

Mueller sent in his excuses to the College, and took to his bed.

Cajetan suggested Dr White, or indeed a doctor of any colour, but Mueller felt well enough by afternoon to sit at the piano and belt out leider till the lamps were lit.

That night, Mueller was an hour making his toilet, leaving the house a little later than usual. He drove like the devil and Cajetan sweated to keep up.

When they stopped, the first thing Muller did was to carry a ladder down from the carriage. It was the folding stepladder from the library.

Cajetan was outraged. When had Mueller transported the ladder out of the library? Why had Cajetan not been informed?

This anarchy so upset Cajetan that the horror of the situation did not sink in until Mueller had almost disappeared over the wall.

The lady was in her balcony, enthusiastically waving her lamp.

Mueller disappeared.

Torn between anger and loyalty, Cajetan left it too long. When he eventually shimmied up the ladder and looked over the wall, he caught sight of his master waiting, lantern in hand, beneath a tree.

Cajetan could have told him that lantern was a bad idea. Mueller was an innocent. He was not used to such excursions. His stint at the Byculla Club had taught Cajetan a great deal. But Mueller had not confided in him, and must therefore take what was coming.

And come it did.

In a few minutes, the front door opened and the lady appeared, carrying her lamp.

Mueller sank to his knees in the light of the lantern and began to sing.

'Gute Nacht Meine Liebling. My favourite!' explained Cajetan, and unleashed the first stanza in a powerful baritone.

Mueller, though, possessed a weak quavering tenor, easily mistaken for the whine of some nocturnal creature.

The lady remained in the doorway either undecided or entranced.

Mueller, now at the penultimate Gute Nacht, let it rip with plosive pulmonary power. The top note was grabbed by the soulful howl of a dog. It was a bulldog, big as a calf. The dog, finding itself in good voice, settled down in the ring of lamplight, and got serious.

Mueller did the one thing he shouldn't have.

He ran.

The dog abandoned its aria and sprang.

Mueller barely made it over the wall with the seat of his pants intact. Luckily he found a foothold, or he would never have scaled the wall.

Cajetan had withdrawn into the shadows. Mueller's intransigence over the stepladder kept him from revealing himself.

The next morning, late for work, Mueller disdained breakfast, and Cajetan gave notice.

'Very well,' said Mueller, nearly felling Cajetan in shock.

That evening, no conversation passed between them.

Mueller swallowed his dinner without noticing what he ate.

Cajetan's heart was near bursting with indignation and sorrow, but he maintained a lofty silence.

Nonetheless, his preoccupation led to a slip of the tongue.

When Mueller wished him good night at eleven as usual, Cajetan replied with Gute Nacht.

Mueller stopped in his tracks.

He held out his hand. 'You would not abandon an old friend, would you, Cajetan?'

'Never!' said Cajetan.

The word was out before he realized, and could not now be taken back.

The first thing Cajetan did after Mueller had left the dining room was to race up to the library. The stepladder was still missing. Mueller was not going to be scared off by a dog.

Unfortunately, while nursing his peeve, Cajetan had foolishly returned the bicycle to his nephew. He considered concealing himself in the carriage, but his was the kind of frame difficult to compact into the boot.

So last night, Cajetan had stayed behind, helplessly watching Mueller vanish into the dark a little past one o'clock. The knowledge that the stepladder had gone too, made sleep impossible. Cajetan debated the wisdom of following Mueller on foot, but sternly told himself that would be of no use. So he composed himself to wait.

He reviewed the week's adventures and came to

a surprising conclusion. Mueller's trysting place was not all that far off. They usually returned around four in the morning. Allowing even an hour for the tryst, that meant no more than an hour's journey either way. The baffling dark and the effort of pedalling blind had confused him. He gave Mueller till four-thirty. After that, he would act.

At five, Mueller had not yet returned.

Cajetan hesitated no longer.

He ran all the way to Seeta Sadan and woke up Ramratan.

'Sahib in danger, hurry!' he implored.

'Is he ill?' Ramratan shouted—for Cajetan was already sprinting back up the road.

From what little he gathered, Ramratan understood their destination was a few miles away.

It was the hour when Nusser made practice runs in his new motor car. It was the only hour when Nergish let him drive.

And so it happened that Cajetan rode in on Mueller's tryst in a Rolls Royce.

But the place was not so easily reached. It was still dark, and somehow the Rolls' powerful headlamps only made it worse. They hurtled in a projection of light, threading the featureless dark with little more than Cajetan's inner compass.

Apart from giving directions, Cajetan was silent.

Ramratan was familiar with that kind of silence. Cajetan would wait to see what transpired before divulging more details.

The sight of a phaeton parked ahead made Cajetan exclaim. 'Mueller Sahib's carriage!'

The headlights then focussed on Mueller himself, sprawled, ready to be flattened by the Rolls.

Nusser slammed on the brakes.

Ramratan thought more of the car's concussion than his own as he extricated himself from the shawls and cushions that had toppled over him, and hurried to join Nusser and Cajetan.

Mueller was alive, but unconscious and bleeding from a head wound. He was also indescribably filthy, his clothes wet and slimy with sludge.

'Home or hospital?' asked Nusser.

'Home,' Cajetan was quick to reply.

* * *

After they had heard Cajetan's story, they looked in on Mueller.

He was awake now, his pulse steadier. He looked at them in surprise, tried to rise, and fell back helplessly on the pillows. Clearly, he had no memory of recent events.

'What to do now?' Cajetan demanded after they gave him the list of things Mueller required.

'Leave that to me,' said Nusser. 'Your Sahib won't want the Hill to hear about this.'

'That's why I called you, and not Dr White. Will you give letter for College?'

'Yes, indeed. Medical leave for a week, don't worry.'

Nusser drove silently. As he dropped off Ramratan, he said, 'One a.m. Be at the gate.'

* * *

Nusser was punctual. They sped through the sleeping streets.

'Darn! We'll need a ladder,' said Ramratan.

'Boot.'

As they approached the scene of the night's

adventure, Nusser grew cautious, even hesitant, at the wheel. The car's sweet purr was barely audible as he pulled up with visible relief.

The wall Cajetan had described was just ahead.

There was a brightness beyond, but little else was discernible.

They lost no time in taking turns at the ladder.

The scene was exactly as Cajetan had described. A brightly lit tree dominated the slumbering grounds. The house was unlit, but not for long.

A window glowed, then darkened.

Then another.

And another.

Presently a woman appeared on the balcony.

By now both men were seated perilously on the wall.

They watched breathlessly as she set down her lamp on the ledge and strained towards the dark.

Ramratan found himself trembling. The woman's face was a blur of brightness, but every line of her body spoke of yearning. She held out her hands in piteous appeal. Her voice rang out into the night.

A movement broke Ramratan's trance.

It was Nusser.

He had jumped down and was running nimbly towards the house.

Ramratan overtook him easily and encircling his friend with an arm of iron, dragged him back to the wall.

Ramratan looked back.

The woman was still there, imploring the dark.

'What was I thinking, Ramratan?' As they parted, he said, 'Best leave it be, eh?'

* * *

Mueller mended slowly.

His internal injuries were nothing serious. Ramratan had let the scalp cut heal without stitches because of the contamination. Above all, they were fearful of tetanus. Nusser had a stock of Behring serum in readiness, but Mueller had shown no alarming signs.

He still had amnesia for that night—indeed for all the preceding nights. When they mentioned the word 'Irrenschloss,' there was no response.

'What does it mean?' demanded Ramratan.

Mueller shrugged. 'Something like castle of madness, I suppose. Why do you want to know?'

Ramratan did not trust his cagey look of innocence. He asked Cajetan to stable the horse at Weston's. Cajetan had already secreted the stepladder.

With these precautions, they thought Mueller was safe.

But Ramratan continued to be uneasy.

He woke at 1 a.m. every night.

It took the comfort of Yashoda's warmth to compel him to stay in bed.

It was a busy week, and he didn't meet Nusser till their usual Thursday session. Nusser looked tired. They were all overworked and underpaid—though in Nusser's case the last could hardly matter. Despite his exhaustion and irritability, there was an exultation in Nusser that Ramratan couldn't explain.

That night, waking again at 1 a.m., he puzzled over why Nusser had looked inspired. As if every thought was spring-loaded and waiting to erupt as song or poetry.

Darn!

Ramratan slid out of bed and found his Raleigh, hoping the boys hadn't messed up the lamp again. The Bridgeport Search Light was Nusser's gift to them, and they couldn't stop monkeying with it day and night. He couldn't blame them, it was delightful to cycle in its lunar glow. Beat the Rolls hollow.

Ramratan pedalled the treacherous kuccha road, the Dunlop tyres were not as cushiony as advertised. He was buoyed by joy alone, delicious with anticipation, comforting in its certainty, joy, joy, joy!

He felt an unaccountable stab of rage when he spotted Nusser's Rolls parked ahead. He alighted and propped the cycle against a tree with slow deliberation, else in his fury he could have hurled it at the Rolls.

And there was Nusser himself, sitting on the wall.

The thought of pushing Nusser off the wall crossed his mind.

Shocked, he pulled himself together with an effort.

Nusser, as yet unconscious of his approach, leaned forward into the dark.

Ramratan climbed the ladder, and took his place on the wall.

They looked at each other, but no sign of recognition passed between them.

In a few minutes all thought of Nusser passed out of Ramratan's mind.

The windows had begun to light up.

His breathing quickened. Each breath seared with exquisite agony, but he could not locate the pain. The roar in his head intensified to a sustained scream that went on and on. He could wait no longer, his very soul was being sucked out of his skin. Part of him had already broken free of that effigy of his self on the wall.

The balcony door opened. The woman did not advance, but waited in the lighted doorway. Slowly, she raised the lamp.

Both men cried out as they recognized her face.

In their haste to claim her, they tangled together in jumping off the wall, and fell on the sharp flinty stones beneath. Nusser was the first to rise and sprint towards the house. Ramratan sprang on him with an enraged roar and knocked him to the ground. They glared at each other with a malevolence neither had felt before.

Ramratan heard himself speak. 'What is she to you?'

'Everything!' Nusser gasped defiantly. 'All the world and more. Let me go, Ramratan! She's waiting for me.'

Ramratan let slip his hold on Nusser's collar. He could no longer see Nusser's face, his eyes were a crush of pain. He fumbled blindly and whispered the impossible. 'Yashoda? She's waiting for you?'

'Yashoda? Have you gone mad? Can't you see who it is?'

'It is Yashoda. How can I mistake her face?' Ramratan's words were lost in sobs.

'Pull yourself together, man! How can it be Yashoda? It is Silloo!'

'Who?'

'You don't know her. Go home, Ramratan. I must go to her. Silloo, I'm coming!' Nusser's voice arched into the night.

The light went out.

The tree was no longer lit either.

Sudden darkness, flat and absolute, pinioned them.

'It was Yashoda,' Ramratan whispered.

'Silloo!' Nusser rasped.

They knew it could be neither woman.

Wordlessly, they climbed over the wall.

Nusser wedged the bicycle in the boot of the Rolls and waited for Ramratan to get in.

Not a word was exchanged on the ride home.

Ramratan raced upstairs.

Yashoda was asleep in their bed, hand out-flung, seeking him.

* * *

By midmorning Ramratan decided he owed Nusser an apology. Perhaps Nusser felt the same, for they collided in the hospital corridor.

'There you are! I was on my way to your office.'

'And I to yours.'

They sat down in the space Ramratan dignified as his office.

'Don't,' Nusser said as Ramratan began to speak.

'Don't what?'

'Don't explain.'

'Can't.'

'Exactly.'

'We each saw—'

'—a different woman.'

'You think Mueller too?'

'Oh yes. Beyond any doubt.'

'Should we warn him?'

Nusser shrugged. What, after all, could they say?

* * *

As it turned out, they should have said something.

That night, Mueller went missing.

Cajetan burst into Seeta Sadan minutes past midnight. He had looked in on Sahib just now, and found the bed empty. Mueller had no carriage, so he must have set out on foot. Cajetan did not try pursuit, thinking it better done by Sahib's friends, although they were only natives. Besides, Nusser Sahib was a magistrate.

'And drives a Rolls Royce. Let's get him.'

Ramratan wondered if the Rolls was in the garage. It

was, with Nusser's chauffeur Wilson snoring in the back seat. Evidently, Nusser had put him there as insurance against himself.

Nusser got Wilson to drive. No more risks.

Mueller was rescued without much difficulty. He was on foot, singing rather drunkenly, and swinging a lantern.

Wedged between Ramratan and Nusser in the back seat, Mueller sobbed all the way home.

* * *

Cajetan served a cold breakfast and gave notice.

When he had cleared the table, Ramratan asked, 'Mueller, who was that woman?'

'Eh? What woman?'

Patiently, they told Mueller everything, starting with his escapades a fortnight ago.

'It's not that I disbelieve you,' Mueller said slowly. 'But I want you to know she was not either of the ladies you mentioned. I've known her intimately—I'd know her anywhere.'

'What is her name?'

'Oh, you can't possibly have heard of her. She's Austrian. Emma. She's called Emma.' Mueller made the two syllables of the name sound like a descant.

'Don't take her name, Sahib,' said Cajetan with menace.

'Emma?'

'Don't call her by that name! Don't take her name! Don't also take a wrong name!' Cajetan glowered. 'I have given notice, so I am no longer your servant. Don't take her name!'

Ramratan put his hand on Cajetan's shoulder. The man felt like a mass of jelly. His cushiony shoulders wobbled in distress.

'You saw her too, didn't you?' Ramratan asked
quietly.

'Every time.' The words broke out in a wail. 'Every
time! I saw Sahib running after her! After my girl! My
Delphine! What can I do but give notice? My Delphine,
lost so many years ago—and now only Sahib can find
her? After all, this Cajetan has roamed everywhere,
looking till he's become old and mad? And now this—
this Professor—finds my Delphine?'

'Sit down Cajetan.' Mueller held out his hand and
led the sobbing man to a chair. 'I was not after your
Delphine. I saw my Emma. My two friends saw two
other women. And yet it was all the same woman—'

'What then, Sahib? Have we all gone mad? What is
that? Bhoot bangla?'

'Irrenschloss,' Ramratan said.

* * *

'Irrenschloss.' Ratan repeated with a sense of recognition.

The painting receded, shrank to a small square on the wall.

The lights came on to diminish the Mondrian abstract
into a small and dingy space.

There was a strong aroma of tea. The rain had stopped.

Time to go home to Nandanvan.

Waiting on the balcony, Radhika would be scanning the
road for his return.

Summmum Bonum

Adel Surveyor broke the anxious silence.

'It is impossible to map the brain,' he said.

The subject of their anxiety was in the next room.

Ratan had invited them to dinner for the sole purpose of understanding his father's condition, and the first hour had been disappointing.

Arjun Oak was taking a nap now, but he would soon rejoin the party.

Of the five guests, Ratan counted only Radhakrishnan as a friend. Raki was no neurologist—he was Ratan's wild card. Adel was a neuropathologist. Sarah Thomas and Jitendar Pal were neurologists, and Zakir Shah was a professor of linguistics.

'Impossible,' Adel repeated. 'There is no such thing as a brain atlas.'

'What about all those pretty diagrams I was weaned on?' Zakir protested.

'They're just pretty diagrams.'

'Oh no, they work,' disagreed Sarah. 'When there's no imaging available, how would I make a diagnosis without those maps?'

'Agreed, they're fine for locating lesions in a stroke. You can map the brain's blood supply, but you cannot map the brain.'

'You'll have to explain that,' said Zakir.

'Listen, if I want to map one mini-column of grey matter, say, a vertical cut from the surface of the cortex to the white matter—that's about 2,000 by 50 microns. Remember, one micron is one-thousandth of a millimeter—can you guess how many sections I'd have to make?'

* * *

'A million?'

* * *

Ramratan had kept up a disapproving buzz all evening, resentful if not downright rude.

'About a hundred?' ventured Zakir.

'Two million. Now tell me, is that even possible? Does anyone have a pin? I want a pin.'

Ratan got him one.

'A bit of cerebral cortex the size of this pin-head has about 30,000 neurons, and—wait for it—one hundred million synapses. So what do we map? How can we even begin to guess what these connections mean.'

'So we don't, cannot, know how the brain is wired?' asked Radhakrishnan.

'Yes. That's about it.'

'Not cell to cell, perhaps,' Jitendar Pal intervened. 'But in general terms we do have a fair idea.'

'A fair idea isn't good enough for me,' said Zakir. 'You can't tell a linguist you don't know where words come from. I thought you guys had cracked it all after Fox P2.'

'What is Fox P2?'

'And God said let there be language,' Adel declaimed. 'FOXP2 keeps Zakir in business. But, it's just a gene, Myrna Gopnik's grammar gene.'

'It gave us language, right?' Radhakrishnan's question had all the trust of a child addressing a conjuror—the magical finish was a certainty, the method irrelevant.

'It gave us languages,' corrected Zakir. 'About seven thousand of them.'

'That's the problem,' said Jitendar. 'Six thousand ninety-nine of them should be banned for the higher good.'

'Which one will you retain?' Raki's voice held a dangerous edge.

It was always a bad idea to talk language with him.

Jitendar answered at once, 'Mother tongue.'

'Yours or mine?'

'Mine, of course. Why should it be yours?'

Adel erupted in laughter.

Jitendar looked irritated as the others joined in. 'Let's put our feelings aside for the moment,' he said. 'It is a simple matter of deciding what you live for. Is it for yourself, or for the higher good?'

'I don't understand.' Raki frowned. 'How can your mother tongue supersede mine for the higher good?'

'Because it is the closest spoken language to Sanskrit, the oldest, purest, language in the world.'

'Who said so?'

'Do you mean to say Sanskrit is the ur-language, the one hardwired in the brain?' asked Adel. 'You think such a primitive language exists? Arjun Uncle here, for instance, has lost all words. You think we should be able to mine some Sanskrit out of his brain?'

'First, I resent you calling Sanskrit primitive. It is the oldest language but it is very sophisticated. Your second question is better answered by Zakir. You're a linguist, aren't you?'

'Linguist enough to know Sanskrit is far from being the oldest language,' Zakir rejoined.

'But the others haven't survived, have they? Every human language spoken on the planet has some degree of Sanskrit.'

'Mine doesn't,' said Raki.

'Then you better learn.'

'For the higher good?'

'You said that before.' Sarah turned on her colleague. 'What exactly is this higher good?'

Before dinner, Arjun had been part of the company. Their attempts to engage him in conversation had failed. He had uttered just one word in the course of the evening. It was neither question nor response. It had arrived during one of those embarrassing lulls in conversation where polite strangers cudgel their brains for something new, and with a bright air of discovery, dazzle with an inanity that is snapped up in sheer relief.

Arjun had said, 'Hawk.'

This caused a flurry.

Had he said Block?

They regrouped hastily, in case someone was blocking his view.

Or, had he said Lock?

Somebody checked the front door.

Or, had it been a throaty sound, a mere strangled cough?

No, it was definitely *Hawk*.

Arjun responded to all this activity with a slight shake of his head.

Ratan understood this to mean he had had enough.

'Time for your nap,' he suggested and was rewarded with a smile. When he returned after making Arjun comfortable, they were discussing the reparative powers of music. Dinner followed, and distracted them from their failed venture on Arjun's brain. Now they returned to Arjun's solitaire.

What had they been talking about when he said, 'Hawk'?

Oh yes, that eternal topic—the frustrations of medical practice. That's when Jitendar had come up with his theory.

'So much of our power is wasted,' Jitendar had said. 'We only treat the sick. Any quack can do that. There has to be some higher good.'

'Better nutrition? Immunity boost? That sort of thing?' asked Sarah.

'Not at all. We must use our power for scientific change.'

'Power?' Ratan was surprised. 'Doctors aren't powerful people.'

'That's because you're only a microbiologist.'

'He possesses the most deadly arsenal,' Adel pointed out. 'Biowar and—boom!'

'Why must you equate power with violence? It can be benevolent too,' said Sarah. 'We have a lot of power to do good during disasters, epidemics, in war zones—'

'No, those are circumstances where our training is helpful. We should use our power to improve humanity.'

'Vaccines?'

'No, no. We should be able to shape a life from its very inception.'

'Conception.'

'No, inception. The gleam in the eye.'

'Oh that's being done. You can order your baby by catalogue.'

'Yes, and then what? You still have to shape its life.'

'That's what parents are for. Why does a healthy child need a doctor?'

'For the higher good. We can weed out weaknesses and foster strengths. We can return humanity to its purest, highest, form. Only we doctors can do that. We must organize and empower ourselves for the higher good. Not schools, but laboratories, where children are cultured in body, mind and spirit.'

It was at this point that Arjun had said, 'Hawk.'

* * *

'Before Jitendar returns us to the higher good, what's the word on my dad?' asked Ratan. 'I know you haven't had much of an opportunity to judge the way he communicates. I can tell you he searches and strains for words, and perhaps comes up with one or two every day. He's still very far from speech, but of late he does understand more. So I do think he's recovering.'

'Does he understand more or do you understand better?' Raki asked.

Everybody laughed.

Raki was serious. 'When my boys were babies I had to learn their language before I could teach them mine.'

'You could have saved yourself the trouble,' said Zakir. 'Babies learn before you can blink. Sometimes two languages, even two dissimilar languages.'

'Three dissimilar languages, in my case. Marathi, Tamizh, English, and now they're talking Hindi as well.'

'How old are they?'

'Five.'

'And the younger ones?'

'They're all five. Triplets.'

'Three kids speaking three languages all at once—I'd never survive it!' Adel cried.

'They have secret languages too. They make up a new one every week and forget the others. It sounds like gibberish, but listen closely, and you can crack the logic. It is strange how easily they invent—and other kids catch on quickly too, so it's not just my boys.'

'No. There is a critical period during which the brain learns very fast. New connections and pathways are formed, I'm told,' Zakir deferred to Adel.

Adel shrugged. 'I wouldn't know about that. I take the brain lightly, in very thin slices.'

'Ratan, to answer your question, I think Radhakrishnan has a point,' said Sarah. 'Perhaps in a complicated way you could even be delaying your father's recovery by taking away his need to verbalize by understanding him.'

'I didn't mean anything of that sort!' Raki snapped.

'No, but I do. When your father returns, I'd like to try a small experiment.'

'Try,' suggested Jitendar. 'But I can tell you it is a wasted effort. Ratan, you're fooling yourself. If you step out of your role as son you'll see what the rest of us can. Your father's aphasia's global. It extends from the lack of comprehension to a loss of words. A total shutdown. He can't understand us. We can't understand him.'

'So where do you locate his lesion on the brain atlas?'

'All Wernicke aphasias are located to temporal lobe defects—'

'Those are lexical—where the patient loses nouns,' explained Sarah.

'Exactly. All Broca aphasias are frontal-subcortical—the patient loses grammar. Your father appears to have lost both. If you ask me, I'd say we're looking at not just a speechless brain, but a wordless one. Besides, I don't think he's registering much of what's going on around him.'

'I disagree,' Adel said. 'His eyes were following the conversation.'

'You can think so if it makes you feel better. My daughter says that about our dog. You and I know a dog's brain cannot verbalize.'

'But dogs do respond to music,' said Zakir, beginning a lengthy anecdote during which Ratan made his escape.

* * *

Arjun was awake. His eyes shone with excitement when Ratan asked if he would like to join the others.

When Ratan was helping him into the chair, Arjun gripped his hand convulsively and said, 'Hawk.'

'Hawk?'

Arjun nodded. The light went out of his eyes. Ratan felt him tremble.

The word was English. Ratan seemed to know that instinctively, although logically, it could have been any language.

'The bird?' asked Ratan.

No.

'Predator?'

Yes.

That was confusing.

* * *

'Not at all. The boy remembers it. I wished him to forget. I had forgotten it myself, until this moment, till he spoke the name.'

* * *

It was a name, then—*Hawk*. 'British?'

But Arjun had slid back into a melancholic abstraction.

* * *

'Not Hawk. Hoche. German.'

* * *

Ramratan's rage was a shudder in Ratan's skin, much like Arjun's tremor a minute ago.

Ratan wrote HOCHE on a piece of paper and showed it to Arjun.

Yes.

Then Arjun raised his eyes to signify he wanted to join the company.

* * *

In Ratan's absence, they seemed to have conspired to a plan of action.

Adel and Jitendar quickly moved their chairs to flank Arjun's wheelchair. Sarah moved forward to cut off Ratan from Arjun's view.

Raki's eyes transmitted discomfort.

Sarah began to converse with the other two in a low murmur and included Arjun in the exchange.

Arjun made no response.

Across the room, Ratan could feel his father's gathering urgency. Or was it his own?

* * *

Let the boy speak!

* * *

Despite knowing Ramratan would always see Arjun as his grandson, Ratan found it worrying. Rather too often, he had caught himself doing the same. Now Arjun's pleading look made him say, 'I think my father wants to say something.'

'Well, that's what we're all hoping for,' said Sarah. 'So if you'll leave the room for a few minutes, Ratan, I'm sure he'll say it.'

'No, that will distress him,' Zakir and Raki spoke in unison.

Sarah demurred. 'Your call, Ratan.'

Ratan was perplexed. He had, after all, invited these experts to help his father, and now he was getting in their way.

* * *

'Oh really? Let the boy speak!'

* * *

So Ratan said, 'Hoche?'

Yes.

Arjun looked at Jitendar.

'You want to me to say that to him? Hoche?'

Yes.

'Jitendar, Hoche is a German name. Mean anything to you?'

Jitendar grimaced.

Sarah rolled her eyes.

Ratan felt helpless before their belligerence.

'Ratan, leave it for now,' Zakir placated. 'Maybe Jitendar can google Hoche and see if that helps.'

'On the other hand, Ratan, we're learning from you.' It was Adel who spoke now. 'You seem to be able to communicate without words.'

His voice startled Arjun. He seemed taken aback, even alarmed.

Ratan realized Adel had unwittingly used the same tone as Nusser. Meeting Adel had been accidental—he hadn't told Adel that he was on intimate terms with his great-grandfather. He had been careful not to mention his surname while introducing Adel. Yet, Arjun had spotted the connection and was projecting a question that could not be evaded.

'You recognize him, Baba, don't you? Nusserwanji?'

Arjun's face lit up with pleasure. He stretched out a trembling hand towards Adel. Tears filled his eyes. His lips moved soundlessly.

'He looks like Nusserwanji?'

Yes. Arjun laughed. It was an amazingly boyish laugh. For a moment Ratan was certain not just he, but the entire room could see Ramratan's ten-year-old grandson.

Adel, meanwhile, was quite confounded. Finally he asked, 'Who is Nusserwanji?'

* * *

'Certainly looks like Nusser. A rough cut. Ask him if he knows Nusser.'

* * *

Obediently, Ratan asked, 'Dr Nusserwanji Surveyor—any relation? Your great-grandfather, perhaps?'

'Yes—so I've heard, but I don't know anything about him.'

* * *

'He wouldn't.'

* * *

Raki was on tenterhooks, suddenly deeply interested in the ceiling, knowing he was about to glimpse Ratan's other life.

'My father knew Nusserwanji very well. He says you resemble him.' It was the best Ratan could manage. He knew that Arjun saw not this young man of thirty, but the ageing man of sixty-five he remembered.

'I'm afraid nobody in our family knows very much about him.' Adel sounded embarrassed.

'My father was raised by his grandfather, and Nusserwanji was a close friend.' That was as far as Ratan was prepared to go.

Arjun said 'Hoche' again, and looked at Jitendar as he did so.

'Gosh, I didn't realize it was so late,' blustered Sarah Thomas. 'We really must be going.'

Arjun seemed to strain every muscle in concentration. They fell silent, watching him. With great effort, and with even greater hesitation, Arjun said, *'Daadu?'*

* * *

1933

'Daadu?' It wasn't often that Arjun addressed him so hesitatingly, so Ramratan kept up the wall of newspaper between them and waited.

'Daadu?'

'Hmm?'

'You have to take me there.'

'All right. Where?'

'Gopal's school.'

Ramratan put down the newspaper. 'I thought we decided that matter was closed.'

'You said all right just now. You said it. You can't break your word.'

'I did say all right, but that was before you told me where.'

'Then you should have asked first.'

'I suppose so. Do you remember why we decided the matter was closed?'

'Yes, I do. And that's exactly why we have to go now. Today. At once.'

'Says who?'

'Gopal.'

With a furtive look over his shoulder, Arjun handed his grandfather a crumpled piece of paper.

Ramratan looked at it warily. 'Secret?'

Arjun nodded.

In the matter of Gopal, Yashoda was likely to be dangerous.

The letter was better read behind the wall of newspaper. It was brief.

Arjun,

ResQ please us. Lyf or deth with sp. injxn. Not joking.

Bakul got blue ticket today.

Come fast.

Yr best frend,

Gopal Madhukar Shinde

'And you got this letter—how?'

'Tatoba gave it to me.'

Tatoba had a corner in the vegetable market where he sold fresh produce from his land in Vasai. Tatoba's basket was plundered clean of ash gourd, pumpkin, snake gourd and yams long before noon, but he always kept back a small stash of Rajali plantains, making certain to display them, temptingly, at five o'clock when Ramratan passed by on his evening stroll.

'So this school is in Vasai, is it?' Ramratan asked.

'Agashi. Tatoba knows the place. If we leave now, we
can get the two o'clock train.'

'And what are we going to tell Ajji?'

'You'll think of something, easy! Can I have a rupee?'

'A rupee? No. What for?'

'Tatoba wants it for bringing the letter.'

'Right. I'll give it to Tatoba myself.'

Ramratan gave Arjun the newspaper, and left the
house. Savoury aromas enticed, but he avoided the
temptation to delay meeting Tatoba till after lunch.
Yashoda would winkle the story out of him in no time.

He had never been at ease with the Gopal situation.
It was an unlikely friendship for Arjun. Gopal was a shy
child who looked permanently terrified. It was easy to
see why he worshipped Arjun, but for the life of him
Ramratan couldn't see what Arjun saw in Gopal. The
two were inseparable. At first, when Arjun brought him
home, Gopal had cowered uneasily on the porch. He
wouldn't come indoors. A few visits later, when Yashoda
set a plate for him alongside Arjun's, he refused to
enter the kitchen. Yashoda served both children their
meal out in the corridor.

'He's not allowed in the kitchen at home,' Arjun
explained later.

'Why not?'

'His mother won't let him. Or Bakul. Bakul doesn't
talk much.'

'How old is Bakul?'

'He's small.'

Gradually, it became evident that the two children
were tormented by their stepmother.

'Come, Arjun, let's walk Gopal home,' he suggested
the next evening.

Gopal didn't look too glad of it. He whispered to

Arjun who looked embarrassed. Ramratan walked on, swinging his cane.

Arjun sidled up and spoke in a fierce whisper, 'If we go to his house, his mother will beat him.'

'Gopal, I have business with your father,' Ramratan said.

'He's not here. He's gone to Indore.'

'When will he be back?'

Gopal shook his head miserably.

To Ramratan's surprise, the house was large and modern. A brass plate announced Dr Madhukar Shinde.

'So your father is a doctor, Gopal?'

'Yes, but he can't make Bakul well.'

Bakul came running towards the gate. He was a sickly looking child of about three—but when he got closer, Ramratan realized he was older, about five or six. Above the filthy shorts, his puny torso was covered with purple smudges.

A fat young woman burst out of the house screaming. 'Where have you disappeared, you idiot? I'm coming after you with red hot tongs!'

And she had them too, a mean pair of iron tongs that she clicked menacingly as she looked about for Bakul, who by now, was crouched in the shadows.

Catching sight of them at the gate, she bustled belligerently. 'Who are these people, Gopal? And where have you been, you cadaver?'

'I am Dr Oak,' said Ramratan. 'Is Dr Shinde at home?'

'No.'

'When can I meet him?'

'How do I know? Come inside, you rogue, and find that idiot brother of yours!'

She grabbed Gopal and with a shove sent him spinning to the ground. Then, with a stony glare at

Ramratan, she stalked back into the house, dragging Gopal in behind her.

The matter didn't end there.

Arjun brought Gopal home with him almost every day. Yashoda was tender with him, and it was heartening to see the sorrow lift from the small pale face. But in the midst of frolic, Gopal would suddenly turn grave and listless when it was time to go home.

'It is because of Bakul,' Arjun told them. 'They're going to send him away.'

The next day, Arjun looked miserable when he came home from school.

'Father Brendan again?' Ramratan asked.

'No, I got ten out of ten in that test.'

'Excellent. What's troubling you, child?'

Arjun was a boy who almost never cried—the last time, Ramratan recollected, was when he was three. But he was weeping now. Not the angry sobs of a child, but the silent bitter tears of a man.

It was Gopal. He was going away too—at least, that's what he had decided. They were sending away Bakul.

'I go where Bakul goes,' Gopal stated. 'No question about that. I go with him, always. Nobody can take him away from me.'

'He's such a little fellow.' Arjun wept. 'How can he fight them?'

That evening there was a crisis.

It was not yet dark. Ramratan was in his study, Yashoda and Arjun were on the porch, intent on a game of Wagh-Bakri.

A strident cry shattered the peace.

'Ai, you whore, what have you done with the boy?'

Gopal's mother was rattling the gate, raising her voice and keeping up an endless stream of invective directed at Yashoda.

Before Ramratan could rush downstairs, Yashoda had walked to the gate.

'Where is he, you shrivelled crone?' the woman railed. 'Is this how you live your life? Robbing the children of others, you miserable widow? You whore!'

Arjun flung himself on her, butted her in the stomach, and knocked the wind out of her.

Yashoda dragged him off the screaming woman.

'Gopal is not here,' she answered calmly. 'If he is lost, my husband will get a constable to look for him.'

'A fine one you are to talk of the police. You should have been hanged long ago.' The woman was full of contempt. 'Everybody knows your story.'

'Get out of here before I break your neck!' Ramratan said with cold menace. 'I will send the police to your house.'

'Come anywhere near the boy again, and I'll throw his corpse right at your gate. Him and his idiot brother's too. Let's see whom the police will want then!'

And, with a few more insults, she took off.

* * *

Yashoda had her arms tight around Arjun to keep him from flying at the woman again. But Arjun was inconsolable.

'Why did she say those horrible things? Is she mad?'

'She is as sane as sane can get,' sighed Ramratan.

The next morning, Gopal turned up at school as if nothing had happened. Arjun found it difficult to speak with him. He told Yashoda they weren't friends anymore.

'Perhaps that's for the best.'

But it wasn't something they could let go.

Ramratan spoke in confidence with Father Vivian, who was only his old buddy Bosco turned Jesuit.

'Not a thing we can do,' Bosco said flatly. 'The class teacher reports the child comes to school with bruises, or a black eye, and by eleven o'clock falls asleep at his desk. What can we do? If we talk to the child they'll only accuse us of trying to convert him. So I let the child be—at least he has this refuge. If he falls back in school work, we'll pull him through. Meanwhile he has friends to nourish his soul.'

Ramratan tried several times to dig up some information about the mysterious Madhukar Shinde, but nobody seemed to know where he practised, or what kind of doctor he was. Everybody, though, knew his loud wife, and the children were objects of general pity.

'None of which helps Gopal.'

'Gopal says his father is putting Bakul in a special school,' Arjun announced. 'They're going to map his brain. And Gopal's too. Then they'll find out what's wrong with them.'

'There is nothing wrong with Gopal's brain,' said Yashoda.

'His father says there is. That's why his mother hates him. But she's not his real mother, so it is only natural.'

'What's natural?'

'She can't possibly love them, can she? They're not her children.'

Arjun couldn't possibly have guessed the hurt he caused Ramratan at that moment.

'I'll tell you something about that later,' said Yashoda. 'For the moment, Arjun, we must let Gopal alone.'

'Why?'

'Because if we don't, he's going to get hurt. If we let him alone, he'll know how to fight his way out. And who knows, this school might be a better place than home.'

'You don't really believe that, do you?'

'I believe that you will always be Gopal's friend. Which means that you'll do what's best for him, even if it may not be what you want to do. Think about it.'

Two days later, Arjun helplessly watched Gopal and Bakul get into a rekla with their father and then they were gone.

As Ramratan left the house in search of Tatoba, he decided he would leave Arjun behind if he decided to go to Agashi. What if the child's note stated the plain truth? Through his long career as police surgeon he had supped full on horrors. Best keep Arjun out of it all.

Tatoba hurriedly put out a bunch of plantains as he caught sight of Ramratan.

'No Rajali today, Tatya. Tell me about the letter you gave my boy.'

Tatya whined a bit, made the usual disclaimers, but Ramratan's stern manner soon had him telling the truth.

The school was adjacent to his farm. When he went to pick vegetables as usual at four in the morning, a small boy had crept up to him. Like the other children in the school, this one too looked permanently hungry, and Tatya was about to cane him for stealing tomatoes when the boy whispered, 'Don't beat me Kaka, not if you want a rupee.'

Now who can say no to a rupee that early in the morning?

'"If you carry a letter to my friend, he'll give you a rupee," the boy said. That won't do, I said. Give me a rupee and I'll carry that letter. "I have no money," he said, "but my friend's grandfather will give you a rupee." And then he mentioned your name, and I knew I could be certain of that rupee.' Tatya's smile dripped with cupidity.

'What do you know about that school, Tatya?'

'I'm not sure it is a school. More like a hospital.'

'Why, are the children ill?'

'Not ill, not exactly, but—lacking. Some are lame. One or two are blind. The teacher is very tip-top. Gora, but not Ingreji.' Tatya made a harsh gargling sound. 'Talks like that. And the headmaster also talks like that, even though he is Brahmin, a regular pandit, but in suit-boot.'

'I see. What about the children? You said they looked permanently hungry.'

'Weak. Weak ones don't last, do they?'

'They don't last in that school?'

'At least four or five go every week.'

'Every week?'

'More, sometimes.'

'Take me there, will you? What time do you leave?'

'Five-thirty, usually. But only because I wait for you to take your stroll.'

'Consider your plantains sold today. Now take your basket to my house with this note for my wife, and get back here as quick as you can.'

Hoping Yashoda had enough cash in the house to pay for Tatya's goods, he dashed off a note saying he was called away urgently on a police matter and would be back at sunset. She would read between the lines, of course.

'Don't say anything to my boy, just get back here quickly.'

Tatya took a little longer than expected. Yashoda's packed lunch explained the delay.

He ate in the shade of a peepal, Tatya having left him to smoke a bidi.

When he returned, Ramratan did nothing encourage conversation. Tatya's indifference to the child's plight enraged him. Thankfully, once they had climbed into the goods' compartment, Tatya placed his basket on the rack and stretched out for a nap.

Two hours later, Tatya pointed out a cottage on the horizon. They had walked several miles from the railway station. Ramratan's calves ached and his head throbbed, sure signs of his blood pressure rising.

The school still looked a mile away.

Tatya offered him a ride back to the station when he was done at the school. His son would be back by then with the bullock cart.

It was nearing five.

The school had high walls, spiked with glass. Tatya said there was a fence around the banana plantation in the backyard. The boys crept through that to his farm. Occasionally, he missed tomatoes.

'How long has this school been here?' asked Ramratan. 'The cottage is old, but the wall is new.'

'Six months. Cottage belonged to a Parsi family, they used to come here on weekends. Hoke bought it off them.'

'Hoke? What kind of name is that?'

'That sahib's name, I think. Hoke Brahmin Arya Pathshala, it is called.'

'Really? Is the Sahib there all the time?'

'Yes. He built a cabin for himself in the compound. They don't let us folk in through the front gate, but they have to live among us, right? So there's a gate through that fence at the back.'

Ramratan had no plan of action. All he could do was either march in through the front gate and demand to see Hoke, or sneak in through the fence and kidnap Gopal and Bakul. The second was more appealing, but it wouldn't solve anything for the children.

The front gate, then.

He was in luck.

The German was on the porch, smoking a pipe.

The place was silent to the point of desolation.

A cold fist of fear closed in on Ramratan.

Were the children all dead?

The German stayed where he was, insolently blowing smoke rings skywards.

Cursing inwardly, Ramratan introduced himself.

'What can we do for you, Dr Oak?'

'I've heard a lot about your school and its methods,' he began cautiously.

'Really? Where did you hear this?'

'From my good friend Dr Madhukar Shinde. I believe his sons are pupils here.'

The name acted like magic. The German dropped his hauteur, and welcomed Ramratan into his office.

'Do I have the pleasure of addressing Herr Hoke?'

'Oh, no, no! I'm sorry if Dr Shinde has led you to believe so. I'm plain Schmidt.'

Wouldn't you be? thought Ramratan.

'Of course, Professor Alfred Hoche is our inspiration. Dr Shinde has discussed his ideas with you?'

'Some of them, yes,' Ramratan admitted with hesitation. 'They sparked my curiosity. I would like to know more. I would like to see how you apply them here in this school.'

'Modest beginnings, Dr Oak, but we try. You are a medical doctor?'

'Pathologist.'

'Excellent. You will then be very interested in our investigations on brain mapping.'

'Really? Craniometry, I suppose?'

'I see you're very well informed. No, Professor

Hoche's methods don't hold with craniometrics as sufficiently accurate.'

'Accurate for what?'

'As an index of intellectual capacity. Present and future. Particularly future.'

'In adulthood, you mean?'

'Indeed, I do not. A child's future is more than adulthood. It is posterity.'

'Of course.'

'Our Dr Pandit is out, at present, or he would explain this to you better, in your own idiom.'

'Yours works just fine with me, Herr Schmidt. Pray continue.'

'Dr Oak. Brahmin, I presume?'

'I'm no pandit, if that's what you're asking.'

'Not at all. You are, by birth, a Brahmin?'

'By birth, yes. But that hardly qualifies me for such a title. It must be earned by striving for enlightenment.'

'We feel that may not be so. We feel your brain is born to a privileged status. Our aim here is to weed out the degenerates.'

'By degenerates you mean—'

'Those who do not qualify.'

'I see,' said Ramratan. But he did not see at all.

'Unfortunately, you've dropped in at an inconvenient time. The children are all asleep.'

'Surely, it is a little early for bedtime?'

'They are woken long before dawn. Their routine is very rigorous. They need the rest.'

'Of course. I wonder if I may call on you tomorrow morning, then?' The words were out before he had thought them over.

'You would be very welcome.'

'How are Dr Shinde's sons?'

'The older one, Gopal, I have some hopes for. You can watch the procedure tomorrow. The younger one shows too many signs of degeneracy.'

Ramratan didn't ask how a child of five could possibly be a degenerate. He concentrated his energies on remaining where he was when every instinct urged him to flee.

'Madhukar said something about—about the child qualifying for a blue ticket—'

'Did he? We generally advise parents not to discuss these things. Seeing that you are interested—I take it there is a child in question? A grandchild, perhaps?'

'Yes.' Ramratan suppressed a shudder.

'Imbecile?'

It was all he could do to keep from smashing his fist into the rascal's skull. He remained quiet.

'I understand. Why not read a little about our ideas first?'

'Is there some material I can borrow? I will be certain to return it tomorrow morning.'

Without further ado, Schmidt took out a dog-eared volume from the cupboard behind him.

'Not a very good translation, I'm afraid. Perhaps you read German?'

'I have only two languages, Marathi and English. More than enough for me.'

'What? No Sanskrit?'

'I'm afraid not.'

'Then you must start learning it immediately.'

'Why?'

'It will be required of you very soon.'

His head in a whirl, Ramratan found it difficult to sustain equanimity much longer. Taking the volume with him, he left, promising to return next morning in time for the clinic at eleven.

Forgetting Tatya's offer of a ride, he trudged in a daze to the railway station. He found a bench, opened the book, and sat down stunned.

The terror that had assailed him in the past hour wasn't paranoia.

The book's title was: *Allowing the Destruction of Life Unworthy of Life*.[2]

> *Is there human life which has so far forfeited the character of something entitled to enjoy the protection of the law, that its prolongation represents a perpetual loss of value, both for its bearer and for society as a whole?*

Ramratan read on, telling himself that was Germany. It couldn't be happening here in India.

The train journey home passed in a blur. He walked home from Grant Road station still blinded by the words of Alfred Hoche and Karl Binding.

Yashoda saw his face and let him in without a word. Arjun was asleep.

Ramratan followed her into the kitchen and handed her the book. 'From Gopal's school. Forget dinner. Read this now. Tell me what to do.'

An hour later, Yashoda said, 'We'll need Nusser. You better get him now.'

'You can't be serious. This can't be happening here.'

'Why not? We kill widows and babies, every day, don't we? What's so shocking about killing a few boys?'

'That's not what I meant.'

'No, it is, Ramratan. In your mind sati and infanticide don't count as murder. This is murder. When you go there tomorrow you'll find that all the pupils are boys. Why? Because the girls have been despatched already.'

---

2. *Die Freigabe der Vernichtung Lebensunwerten Lebens.*

'That's cynical.'

'You think so because you're a man. Ask any woman. Now go find Nusser.'

Nusser would be happier listening to the tale at Seeta Sadan.

Yashoda had expected that. A steaming carafe of coffee awaited them. They sat on the dark porch, and listened to Ramratan's story.

'We must get Edwardes,' said Nusser.

S.M. Edwardes, ex-Police Commissioner, had been dead these five years, but somehow they always called the Commissioner Edwardes. The present incumbent, Goodman, was none too intelligent—but he had his uses. He owed Ramratan several favours, not least being the rescue of his son-in-law from a chandol-khana in Safed Gali.

At eleven sharp the next morning, Ramratan presented himself in Schmidt's office. Greetings passed. A studious looking young man was introduced as 'Our brilliant Dr Pandit.'

'Of Bombay University?' enquired Ramratan.

'Class of '16.'

'How did you get so familiar with German science?' The word 'science' stuck in his throat.

'I was at Heidelberg,' said Pandit with great pride.

'They read Hoche there?'

'Hoche and Rüdin and Kraepelin and Kallman. All the great men.'

'Do they all share the same thought?'

'Every doctor in Germany does.'

'Really Pandit, that's an exaggeration.' Schmidt appeared embarrassed. 'The League has about 3,000 doctors, certainly.'

'And they believe—'

'In *Rassenhygiene*. Race Hygiene. You know that pure Aryan stock originated in the Arctic—'

'It did? Who are these pure Aryans?'

'You yourself, Dr Oak, and our stalwart Pandit here. You have maintained your purity by your strict marriage laws. Isn't breaking them often punishable by death?'

'I won't speak for Dr Pandit, but I'm a child of the equator, as impure as that gets, Herr Schmidt.' Ramratan set down his hand as a contrast to Schmidt's white one on the table.

Schmidt smiled. 'The degeneracies of self-domestication. Never mind that. Let's do a little brain mapping.'

'Yes, please, curiosity overcomes politesse.' That would have made Arjun giggle—at the thought of him, Ramratan's hands grew deathly cold.

'In Germany, we are funded by the rich Rockefellers. Or were, till this year. Now it is up to Indian philanthropists to take up the torch. They haven't been lacking, not lacking at all. Bring in the children, Pandit.'

What a pathetic crew then crept in!

Most of the children were below ten, hollow-cheeked, wan. Their eyes were vacant. It made Ramratan suspect they were already dosed with some nostrum. He caught sight of Gopal at the end of the file. The boy had dwindled alarmingly. His nose bled, and he kept staunching the drip with his sleeve. His eyes, though, were alert and observant. He hadn't yet noticed Ramratan. When he did, Ramratan already had a cautionary finger on his lip. The child's eyes leapt with hope, but he quickly looked away. A lifetime of torture at home hadn't taught him to dissemble as swiftly as the past fortnight had.

Mapping the brain proved more arbitrary than Ramratan's worst expectations.

The children's heads were measured with gigantic calipers that induced either desperate attempts at flight or a benumbed resignation even more pitiful.

Schmidt had a terrifying contraption on his desk, all metal arcs, buckles and leather slings. In case you failed to imagine what it was meant for, a poster showed a child's head entrapped in it. A pile of papers printed with tables sat next to this machine.

The procedure was swift.

Each child had a paper with his name on it.

Pandit measured.

Schmidt matched the measurements against the tables. Then he shaded in red or blue a carbon copy of the standard diagram of the brain, and handed it like a trophy to each child.

At the door an attendant separated the children into red and blue streams.

There were fifty boys in all.

Yashoda was right.

No girls.

'What do red and blue signify?' asked Ramratan. He could hardly trust his voice.

'These tables are my own mathematical derivation after observations from Craniometry, Prosopometry, Plastometry, Anthropometry and Somatometry. The blue shading is a diagnosis of complete idiocy. The red indicates strong signs of degeneracy.'

'I see. How do you treat these ailments?'

'As you can imagine, the blue children—Blue Tickets they call themselves—fall into the category of lives unworthy of life. We put them under special nutritional care.'

'That is—you starve them?'

'Caloric restriction to restrain criminal activities is

imposed upon both categories. But Blue Tickets go on to a more advanced management of total deprivation to prepare them for the final solution.'

'The special injection?'

'Indeed.'

'I don't see Shinde's children here. Oh yes, that's his older son, isn't it? Gopal, come here!' Ramratan rapped out the order in as severe a tone as he could manage.

Gopal shuffled up to him, and when Ramratan lifted him up, clamped on to him like a leech.

'Your nutritional care has certainly rid him of undesirable reserves,' observed Ramratan, a little shocked by his own ease with the language of deceit. 'What about the younger boy? May I see Bakul, please? That's the category for my own—candidate.' He could not bring himself to say grandson.

Gopal's tremors ran like aftershocks through Ramratan. He fiercely willed the child to stay alert, but Gopal was beginning to feel floppy.

'Let this be over quickly,' he prayed to whatever god would listen.

Schmidt did not hesitate over the request. He led Ramratan to a vast shed-like interior. A brown curtain partitioned off the segment reserved for the Blue Tickets. The floor was strewn with small bodies in various degrees of exhaustion and collapse.

Schmidt pointed to an emaciated child who seemed asleep.

A closer look told Ramratan that Bakul was comatose. His breath had the queasy sweetness of ketosis. Death was hours away.

'I am a rich man,' Ramratan heard himself say. He was no longer in control. Might as well be led by automatism now. 'I would like to make a large endowment. But before I do so, just one request.'

'Anything. Anything!'

'Most kind. I would personally like to observe the final solution. Bakul is quite ready for it, I think. But I must insist that this be carried out on my premises because I have organized to film the entire procedure. Do not concern yourself about transport. My Rolls awaits.'

Ramratan reached into his coat pocket. 'Here, Herr Schmidt, is my endowment—merely the first installment.'

Ramratan handed him a Bank Order for Rs 50,000.

'Munificent!' gasped Schmidt.

'As I said, it is only the first installment. Now, if you'll permit me—'

Ramratan whistled—the shrill looping whistle of his madcap school days.

Within minutes, the room swarmed with police.

* * *

'We have achieved exactly nothing,' Ramratan said bitterly.

It was two days after the raid on Hoche's School.

Nusser and Ramratan were waiting in the Police Commissioner's office.

The children had been 'rescued'—returned to the homes which had rejected them, and condemned them to incarceration and death.

For Gopal, though, Ramratan hoped for some alleviation. When the police had gone looking for Dr Madhukar Shinde at his residence, a shamefaced man had come out of the darkened bedroom, hastily tucking in his dhotar. The havaldar saw just enough of his averted face to recognize him as the baniya from the store down the street.

'Why are you waiting outside, havaldar sahib?' A teasing voice floated out. 'I'm in here if you want to talk to me.'

Madhukar Shinde had been apprehended in Indore and was due to appear before the Magistrate that afternoon. Once the law had dealt with him, perhaps he would make a better parent. His wife's scandalous ways were common knowledge—now he knew too.

Meanwhile Bakul was recovering in hospital, and Gopal refused to be moved from his bedside.

Ramratan told Arjun that Gopal's school had been shut down.

To Arjun's question, 'When can I see him?' Ramratan had no answer.

'I don't want the child to know any of this evil,' he confessed to Nusser. 'If it means having to lie to him, I will.'

'We'll see.'

They were waiting for Pandit to be brought in. Commissioner Goodman arrived with the air of a man about to break a rule. He cleared his throat. 'There are bound to be some damaging facts—'

'Damaging to whom?'

'To us. That is—'

'To the British Empire?' Nusser helped him out.

'Yes, but they are not the views of the Government.'

'No?'

'Not any more than the views of Dr Pandit are those of Sanskrit gentlemen in general.'

'Did you find the bodies?' asked Ramratan.

The Commissioner looked startled. 'Bodies! Surely you don't think?'

'I noticed a banana plantation in the backyard. At least twenty rows in that small space. You should look there.'

'But—'

'Commissioner, Tatoba reported four or five deaths every week. It was common knowledge. The rate at which Blue Tickets were issued was much higher. We saw at least thirty children being prepared for murder—'

'Murder! Surely that's extreme? Pandit and Schmidt can't be charged with murder. Neglect, starvation, medical malpractice.'

'That's it?'

'That's it.'

They glared at each other, open enemies.

Pandit was brought in.

'I object to these handcuffs,' he argued. 'I'm a medical man, not a common criminal.'

'You are a common criminal, sir, and will be treated as such,' said Goodman. 'I would advise you to answer our questions truthfully.'

'Did I say I won't?'

'We are medical men, too,' Ramratan reminded the Commissioner.

'And we would like to know how he participated in this murderous scheme,' Nusser added.

'That is a matter of opinion. In Germany, in England, in America, they would be shocked to hear you describe our school as 'a murderous scheme.' It is a deeply considered plan for the higher good. Above all, it is Indian! Our varna system is nothing but ancient eugenics. It is Galton's 'judicious marriage' practised over the ages. We still practise it in every part of our country. What's so shocking about it?'

'We don't practice murdering innocents!' Nusser responded hotly.

'No? What about doodh peetha, drowning your infant daughter in sweetened milk? What about sati? Have you looked into Ayurvedic texts and read the advice on

women and children? The whole world does it. We were
doing it in a humane manner.'

'Humane?'

'The injections are painless, I assure you. Specially
developed in the most advanced laboratory in Germany.
Before you ask, every German doctor I know, and I have
worked with the best of them, supports our ideas.'

'Supports, but not practises,' said Ramratan. 'A
great deal of hot air passes for intellectual debate, but
how many consent to getting their hands dirty?'

'You want numbers? 84,525 applications were
received from physicians who wanted to sterilize their
feeble-minded patients.'

'Applications? Is it not against the law?' Ramratan
could not keep the shock out of his voice.

'For the last two years, the Third Reich has had a law
to prevent genetically defective progeny. Chancellor
Hitler has made it possible, and doctors vie with each
other to alleviate the burden on the state. You can trust
my information. I worked there before I came back
home to establish a progressive school with Schmidt.
I wish now I hadn't. To be so misunderstood! Germany
welcomed me. Did you think the school was Schmidt's?
Far from it. It was all my idea. I named it after Hoche.'

'Why Brahmin and Aryan?' asked Nusser.

'Because unlike Germany we already have the purest
of the pure. Worry not, you are included. The Avesta is
another version of the Rig Veda. We only accept pure
Brahmins. We check their gotra and horoscopes back to
the seventh generation.'

'You do, I suppose. It is unlikely Schmidt knew any
such rubbish.'

'Rubbish? You call it rubbish? And you a Brahmin?'

'Bombay is not Germany,' Goodman said tiredly.
'Bombay is British.'

'Britain's not far behind.'

'That's as it may be.'

'No, I think you should know that much of the work in Germany has enthusiastic British support—and American money. Of course, America is much more progressive.'

'Listen to me, Pandit!' Ramratan thundered. 'What gives you the idea we're interested in the ideas of a bunch of German lunatics? You have murdered our children. Don't you dare call yourself a doctor.'

Pandit laughed. 'Would you like to know how many doctors here support us? Shall I show you the waiting list? Shall I tell you how many posh South Bombay clinics have begged for samples of our injection? Everybody except you, it seems, Dr Oak, is interested in the higher good—'

* * *

'—the higher good?'

Jitendar had just asked a question which had a familiar ring.

With some embarrassment Ratan requested him to repeat it.

'I asked you, for the fifth time, what does Hoche have to do with the higher good? I gather that's what your father wishes to tell me.'

'Alfred Hoche?' asked Raki cautiously. 'That Hoche?'

'The very same.'

'Never heard of him,' retorted Jitendar.

'His ideas were very like yours,' said Raki with venom. 'And they were put into practice for the higher good. *Summum bonum*, the highest good.'

'I want to read this. Is he published?'

'Of course.'

'WhatsApp the links to me, please.'

'Just Google *Holocaust*.'

'Sure, I'll look it up. If it is so good it should have gone viral already.'

'The Holocaust, Jitendar!' Sarah was determined to educate. 'The Nazis! Concentration camps! Gas chambers!'

'Yeah. I saw that movie. Real tear-jerker. Cute kid, but I thought the clown was over-rated. Nowadays anybody can get an Oscar. Is that what your father was asking? If I'd seen the movie?'

'He wanted to remind you about how doctors of an earlier age had used their power for the higher good,' said Raki with extreme self control. 'Hoche wrote a book that was very influential. The title is self-explanatory—*Allowing the Destruction of Life Unworthy of Life*.'

'Euthanasia?' Sarah asked.

'If you like euphemisms.'

Ratan decided to fill in the blanks. 'Seventy thousand so called imbeciles were killed by the State. All of these murders were recommended by doctors.'

'This, do not forget, was *before* the Nazis targeted Jews. Imbeciles, cripples, schizophrenics, gypsies, homosexuals—anyone, everyone, who was different.'

'One way of maintaining balance,' persisted Jitendar. 'Darwinism in practice.'

'Oh no. Darwin never thought so. You ought to read him.'

'Where's the time, man?'

'Then do not cite him. Forget Germany. I think the reminder was to us, about the here and now.'

'Racial hygiene, as practised in our midst,' said Ratan. 'Eliminating the Other.'

'Oh come on, Ratan! That's extreme,' Sarah protested.

'Really? Ask Zakir. Ask Radhakrishnan.'

The two named men glared back. Their faces were stone. They could have been twins, so similar were their masks of namelessness.

Jitendar shrugged. 'That's anecdotal.'

'Interesting choice of word.' Zakir broke his silence.

'I mean—that was your experience. It need not be the general experience.'

'Depends on your perception of "general". I think what you're really saying is it happened to *someone else*. Is "general", your kind?' asked Raki.

'True. If something bad happened to you, my sympathies. But I'm not ready to believe it will happen to me. What happened to you, anyway?'

'Raki, Zakir,' Adel intervened. 'You don't have to talk about it.'

'No? Perhaps we do. Since you ask, Jitendar, my father was murdered by Shiv Sena goons in 1966. The reason? He was a Tamizhan. That morning he went out to buy milk. The sight of a man in a veshti was provocation enough. They beat him to death just across the road from our doorstep.'

'And here you are, forty years later, still in Mumbai.'

'This is home. What do I care where my ancestors came from? Their lives are over.'

'I agree,' said Zakir. 'My family was massacred in Ahmadabad. One day, I too will return.'

'I'm sorry, really sorry, guys. But this is still anecdotal.'

Zakir laughed mirthlessly. Disquiet hushed the room. 'Anecdotal? You seem fond of the word. Do you know what it means? A thing unpublished.'

'There is enough Holocaust literature to fill all the libraries on the planet. There is enough about *our* own genocides. Beginning with the Partition, and then perpetrated every year since, in some corner of the subcontinent—India, Pakistan, Bangladesh, Sri Lanka. Every day the papers announce some new atrocity committed for the higher good.'

'Hota hai,' Jitendar shrugged.

'Somewhere else. To someone else.'

'Exactly. And we can't condemn without looking for reasons.'

'I think that's what my father means to say,' said Ratan. 'A doctor's so-called powers may induce him, or her, to rationalize the most abhorrent of crimes for the higher good.'

'Him maybe, never *her*,' Sarah exclaimed.

'Aha. Historically many of those doctors were women. German, British, American,' Raki interjected. 'And not just doctors. That high priestess of literature, Virginia Woolf, she wrote about her visceral disgust for imbeciles and wished them exterminated.'

'You know what I think, Ratan? Medically, I mean? About your father?' Jitendar paused dramatically. He had the attention of the room. 'I think your father's words and gestures mean nothing. You read your own thoughts into them.'

'Yes, I agree.' Sarah gushed. 'When you were out of range, he did not make a sound.'

'That is because you don't understand his language,' said Zakir. 'To you, and to Jitendar, his words are unintelligible. What would you find, Adel, if you mapped their brains?'

Everybody laughed at that, Jitendar loudest of all.

'It's been an interesting evening.' He reached across Arjun and shook hands with Ratan. 'Hang in there, man.'

'Thanks.' Ratan smiled.

'Oh, don't thank me please. I've done nothing. It was just—just—'

'Anecdotal.'

The word startled them into silence.

With exquisite clarity, Arjun spoke again.

'Anecdotal.'

The Neighbourhood of Memory

It is a room cavitated by shade. Recesses, umbrageous fossæ, walls pockmarked with sockets of greater emptiness, and the ornate void of the magnificent bay window. Shut now, its murky panes leave slices of light wavering on the marble floor. Syrupy bright quadrilaterals, soon to diffuse and gild everything as the sun goes down. That westward notion brings with it a proximity to the sea, although he can neither hear nor smell it in here.

'What is this place?' Ratan asked.

She was invisible, covert in one of those recesses. He imagined her smiling as she answered his question.

'Call it the neighbourhood of memory.'

'Must we be quiet, then?'

'I shall be.'

The place lacks furniture. Anyway, he doesn't feel like sitting down.

He looks up at the ceiling, high and vaulted like a ribcage. A wire dangles from a broken light fixture.

He paces about uncertainly trying to get a feel of the place.

The city held many spaces in transit from expansive past into indeterminate future. Most succumbed quickly to commerce or popular culture, their slick newness not disguise but avatar.

This one feels different.

The window looks down on a roofscape. Tides of terracotta trickle towards the horizon, their neap and ebb eternal, disdainful of change.

The market crouches beneath. Fragrant and stinking, flourishing and putrefying, darkened and incandescent, flashy, ragged, dainty, sordid, old and very new, as ambivalent as its stipulation.

The clock tower, the red and white tiling, the bas reliefs made by Lockwood Kipling's industrious students, and the ugly fountain now dry and clogged with paint—all these were dreamed up by that scandalous bully Arthur Crawford for the mems and the sahibs of a dead age. The bullied masses got their voice too, in Jyotiba Phule, and for a while, the market bore his name. It was back to being Crawford Market now, but Jyotiba had his plaque—where had he seen it?

He cannot recall.

Every time he tries to remember the plaque, it is Lockwood Kipling's fountain he sees. Not choked with a thick daub of blue paint and surrounded by boxes of bletting mangoes—

Shooting out chill sprays, it makes a bid for elegance with the kind of grandeur only true ugliness can command.

Ornate, even flamboyant in its cheapness, it draws

sniggers from the crowd. On its painted panels, devis flash their nipples through swirling waves of blue and white.

'Indian rivers,' an educated voice proclaims.

The voice wears a top hat.

Arcs of water glitter. The ringed faces lurid in the glare are sweating excitement.

It is not the fountain.

It is the light.

Electric.

The date announces itself: 1882.

The market is bright when the streets echo with marching. 1914.

Still bright in the dim slow parade of the dead. 1918.

* * *

'Perhaps that's what happened,' said Ratan aloud. 'I built a memory palace.'

She did not ask when.

'Perhaps,' repeated Ratan, 'I used the market as my memory palace.'

He didn't even know what a memory palace was, except that it had to do with clustering things around this locus or that, and then when you recalled a locus, all the bric-à-brac rumbled up with it too. Wishful thinking.

What idiot had dreamed it up?

Cicero.

Chichero, a voice corrected him.

'He had a wart like a chiche on his nose, or on his chin, somewhere visible, for God's sake! Chiche? Channa, Kabuli channa, gram.'

Gram.

He knew not the voice, but the word mattered.

Gram.

A word leafy with meanings, but also rooted in meaning. *To write.*

'No. That's Greek. For chiche-gram, you want the Portuguese for grain. *Grao.* Gram.'

Why now? Why *gram*?

Why did it matter so in here? At this moment in here, in this neighbourhood of memory?

Gram—the word summoned up the sound of marching. The tired spill of stragglers who survived.

Gram brought a gunshot.

A single shot in the centre of the forehead of a sad-faced man.

Ratan had never seen his picture, but he knew the face. No, he knew the man.

He knew the name and imagined his face.

Only the face with its bloodless wound showed above the flag.

He had wrapped the flag around himself. The kind of shroud, the kind of death every Indian felt driven to, now, today. But this man's flag was not the Indian tricolour. It was black, red and white.

It was German, of 1918.

The man's name was Richard Semon.

He belonged here, in the neighbourhood of memory.

Engram, that was Semon's word.

That was Semon's thought.

He had no proof.

It was just a thought, and largely ignored.

Engram [said Semon] was a lasting connection made in the brain to establish memory. This memory trace was a *physical change*. Semon said this, but he knew not its how or why or even its where.

Camillo Golgi and Santiago Ramón y Cajal had spelt out the sane brain in black and white. Alois Alzheimer and Emil Kraepelin had pinned down its madness. Sigmund Freud and Carl Jung had juggled with its phantoms —

And here came an idea, an idea, nothing more, that bridged the abyss between substance and spirit.

All simultaneous excitations…within our organisms form a connected simultaneous complex of excitations which, as such, acts engraphically, that is to say leaves behind it a connected and, to that extent, unified engram-complex.

They all laughed at him.

He riposted loftily:

I should be as able as anyone else to turn out some sort of schematic representation on the model of the diagram of Mendelian determinants in which engrams would be naïvely represented, schematized as tiny particles and conveniently packed together. This would meet the views of those readers whose thirst for causality requires such schematic representation, and who cannot resign themselves to leaving such questions open for the time being. My own conception of inductive science is a different one, and I attribute more value to an honest note of interrogation than to constructions which are only representable through an effort of imagination.

And then, he shot himself.

* * *

Ratan could understand that. One could easily kill oneself over memory.

The very point of memory—*mnemic sensation* in Semon's words—was absence.

Memory was loss. It fed itself endlessly, initiated, driven, sustained and renewed by loss.

Semon's view, that perception formed memory, should have been self-evident, but it wasn't, not in his time.

Semon was certain that perception was more than a single sensation. He discerned it as the theatre of the instant of experience. An opera entire in a blink.

That is as difficult to define today, as it was to Semon a hundred years ago.

Semon could never locate the engram.

* * *

The roofscape was as featureless, as daunting, as a slice of brain under the microscope. Tile upon tile endlessly networked to no evident purpose.

And underneath, the seething agora of sapience.

* * *

The traffic thinned.

Buses and taxis seemed to dissolve into clouds of dust that cleared almost instantly. There were bullock carts now, and a bicycle or two. He heard the clip-clop of horse hooves before he saw a phaeton pass.

The men and women looked different, even if their clothes were familiar—dhoti, pants, nauvari sari.

And how few they were—

He knew the date instinctively.

1905.

He was not yet born—that was still 52 years in the future.

Semon couldn't have explained this memory.

Not unless he could locate the engram.

'You're looking for footholds.' She broke her silence. 'You don't need them. Keep walking.'

* * *

Taking for granted that memory was perception, how would one locate *that*?

In cell assemblies—neurons welded in solidarity across synapses, strengthened by each new firing of impulse. LTP versus LTD.[3] Neuro-jargon which meant that each memory formed new synapses, and perhaps, erased older ones.

The memory engram was the changing synapse. No longer cleft, abyss, emptiness.

More than a spritz of molecules that excite or depress, the synapse was the place of translation where thought became meaning.

So what changed the synapse? What altered permanently to *en*-graph memory?

Memory means more synapses, more receptors, more chemicals, of course. But also cells that show up active and curious to learn.

Not all cells do.

Only inquisitive cells that can be tagged in the laboratory, appear as the memory trace, the engram.

Why only these and not others?

Why only him, and not others?

---

3. Long Term Potentiation [LTP] opposes Long Term Depression [LTD]. In concert, they affect neuronal synaptic plasticity.

Why was he all memory in a world of amnesiacs?

Why not have his brain tagged with optical opsins and see what became conspicuous?

* * *

'You're getting mired in place — '

'No, I'm mired in time.'

'You're looking for the place of time, seeking to define which part of your brain controls your moment in time.'

'Yes. I want to locate the engram.'

'What if it is not one, nor even a bunch of points, in your brain? What if it is everywhere? What if it is nowhere? Will it matter?'

It would matter if he had a stroke. If a part of his brain died. Degenerated. He wouldn't know then where he stood in time.

But now —

'Now. Keep walking.'

'Is that all it is? The journey?'

'Isn't it, always?'

* * *

The engram was not a trace but a thicket of memory.

Last week he was shown fluorescing synapses in the hippocampus — a red and green web of pulsatile thought, vibrating with intent that remained unintelligible.

It had nearly paralyzed him.

The brain stores galaxies. Stray scintillae present themselves as memory.

What happens with the rest that is forgotten? Is it stored in the engram, and awaits retrieval?

Does it wait a lifetime? Two?

Does it make the transit from one skull into a million others, viral, perhaps?

Are we thoughts awaiting retrieval from the universal synapse at the advent of a newer, more complete, intelligence?

* * *

Lights come on outside.

Neons. Sodium vapour. White glare.

The sky fades out and becomes a shadow.

The room darkens. The recesses become patches of pallor.

The roofscape outside is erased by emptiness.

'Closing time.'

Not really. It travels with him.

No matter where or when he is, it will always be the neighbourhood of his memory.

MURDER IN SEVEN ACTS
Kalpana Swaminathan

'The reason that Swaminathan should be read—and is enjoyed by so many—is the sheer delight of her writing. She manages to oscillate between ironic, playful, lyrical and macabre with equal ease.' —Anita Roy in *India Today*

The curiosity of murder unfolds in seven acts.

Since Kalpana Swaminathan's first whodunit was published over ten years ago, Lalli—sixty and silver-haired and tough as nails—has been one of the most memorable detectives in Indian fiction. Lalli returns in this brilliant page-turner, a collection of seven stories, to solve some of the strangest, most complex cases of her career.

The opening act, in which a face keeps reappearing until a crime committed long ago is revealed, is followed by a murder that could be hypothetical—or a reality (Lalli turns to Schrodinger's Cat to find out). In the third act in this unfolding drama, Lalli and Sita are invited to a book-burning which turns out to be murder most foul. And Lalli turns her skills to the world of high fashion when Sita sits next to a serial killer on a bus—but was he killer or victim?

The aptly named Suicide Point in Bombay's suburbs, leads Lalli to a suicide that turns out to be something far more sinister. And an innocuous desk ornament is the clue to a crime most artistically executed. Finally, for connoisseurs of fiction, the curtains come down with a threnody for lost love.